CW00590032

Other (Non-Cupcake) books by Kyell Gold:

Argaea
Volle
The Prisoner's Release and Other Stories
Pendant of Fortune
Shadow of the Father
Weasel Presents

Out of Position
Out of Position
Isolation Play
Divisions
Uncovered
Over Time

Dangerous Spirits
Green Fairy
Red Devil
Black Angel

Other Books
Waterways
In the Doghouse of Justice
The Silver Citcle
X (editor)

Other Cupcakes:

Bridges, by Kyell Gold
The Peculiar Quandary of Simon Canopus Artyle, by Kevin Frane
Science Friction, by Kyell Gold
Dangerous Jade, by foozzzball
Winter Games, by Kyell Gold
Indigo Rain, by Watts Martin
The Mysterious Affair of Giles, by Kyell Gold
Dude, Where's My Fox? by Kyell Gold
Koa of the Drowned Kingdom, by Ryan Campbell
Losing My Religion, by Kyell Gold

The Time He Desires

by Kyell Gold

This is a work of fiction. All characters and events portrayed within are fictitious.

THE TIME HE DESIRES

Copyright 2016 by Kyell Gold

All rights reserved, including the right to reproduce this book, or portions thereof, in any form.

Published by FurPlanet Productions
Dallas, Texas
http://www.furplanet.com

ISBN 978-1-61450-336-1
Printed in the United States of America
First trade paperback edition: December 2016
Cover and all interior art by Kamui

For a cat who taught an old fox and wolf
that it's never too late to change.

"If, in spite of intense supplication, there is a delay in the timing of the Gift [al-'ata], let that not be the cause for your despairing. For He has guaranteed you a response in what He chooses for you, not in what you choose for yourself, and at the time He desires, not the time you desire."

— *The Hikam, Ibn 'Ata'illah, Chapter 1, 6.*

Contents

Chapter One: The Camera

In his younger days, Aziz stood at the pawnshop counter while taking his afternoon tea, proud of his store. But years ago he had suffered a strain in his back; now when the old grandfather clock chimed four, the cheetah sat at the end of the counter, poured mint tea out of the samovar, and luxuriated in his rest. The view out his front window, unlike Aziz himself, had gotten brighter and newer over the two decades he'd owned the pawnshop. Old brownstones had aged and crumbled, then been demolished and partially replaced with bright yellow brick apartment homes, and three years ago those had given way to a "modern living and shopping space," a six-story blue glass and chrome monster that sprawled across two city blocks. The Upper Devos Homeporium (a development of the Vorvarts group) had assured the merchants in the area "increased foot traffic in your neighborhood, bringing more business and property value to the area," and Aziz along with the others on the Upper Devos Business Council had voted to approve the development. They hated those yellow brick things anyway.

But that had been five years ago, and as it happened, the people who'd lived in the yellow brick things, who'd been forced to find somewhere else to live when their buildings had been bought, they had been part of the neighborhood not easily replaced. The people who lived and shopped at the Homeporium generally stayed there, not venturing outside to quaint old Upper Devos, and when they did come into the pawnshop, distinctive in their clean, crisply cut clothes, they gawked about with the air of tourists visiting a historical monument. Aziz's business had fallen off; few of these people were hard up enough to have to pawn their possessions, or interested in buying someone else's memories. If he hadn't expanded into online sales years ago, he would have had to close this shop. Not everyone was so down on the new development; Vorvarts considered the Homeporium a smashing success and was planning to expand it. There were talks of a cineplex, a skating rink, a bowling alley.

The door jingled. Aziz looked up to see a short red fox slipping into the shop, his light blue cotton shirt hanging open over a pair of khaki slacks. He held nothing in his paws, but strode purposefully to the counter as if he were bringing something to sell.

The cheetah stood and frowned slightly, searching his memory. There were plenty of red foxes who had come into the pawnshop over the years, but not so many in the last few years. The red foxes who inhabited the neighborhood now were European, upscale, far too snooty to grace a pawnshop with their presence—the kind who wouldn't live in the Homeporium but would shop nowhere else. But this one was different, definitely one of the longtime residents of Upper Devos or the nearby towns, and yet Aziz did not know him. "Good afternoon, sir," the cheetah said. "How may I help you?"

"Hi," the fox said. "I'm looking for a video camera, a Pawtic R400."

"Of course." Aziz pointed to the back left corner of the store. "We have several on the shelves back here. Newer models than that one, too."

"No. I'm looking for a specific one." The fox looked away and took a breath. "It would have been brought in about a year ago by a cougar named Gerald DeRoot. I have..." He dug into the bag at his side. "I have our marriage certificate and my id, so you know I'm his family."

While he was laying the paper and the driver's license on the table, Aziz kept his demeanor calm. He'd run into married male couples before, and they always made him feel wary but with a vertiginous fascination. Of course, sexual contact with males was haraam, but the couples he knew weren't Muslim. Normally when he encountered a non-Muslim eating pork, for example, or drinking alcohol, or even cheating at cards, he felt only a sense of being other, and not one that bothered him. But back in his home country of Madiyah, homosexual behavior was punishable by death, often brutal and public. This had been an immutable fact of Aziz's life until he was past twenty and stepping off a plane in the States.

Here he had found a different world. He read the newspapers and watched the increasing acceptance of gay people and couples with the memory of his uncle's flight always in his mind. And so, perhaps, he did not look for those people and couples in his everyday life. When the two female fennec foxes who owned the organic grocery store down the block had announced their marriage, he'd been surprised. "You didn't know they were a couple?" Halifa had said with amusement, and Aziz had responded stiffly that he didn't look for such things. But after that there were more marriages and he started to see relationships even outside the wedding announcements.

And then there had been his son.

"Sir?"

Aziz looked down with a start. His paws felt tight. The fox had placed an id on the counter next to a piece of paper, so Aziz stretched his fingers as he examined both. The license identified the fox as Benjamin Tonnen, with an address over on Larchmont. And the piece of paper…

This certifies that Gerald DeRoot and Benjamin Tonnen were joined in marriage on the 2nd day of April, 2011.

The two male names, the joining in marriage…the cheetah's paw shook slightly as he laid the paper down. "You didn't need to bring this," he said. "Anyone may purchase anything in the store."

"Yes, but that camera is really important. If someone else bought it, I was hoping you might let me know who. It's not even the camera. It's the tape. He sold it with the tape still in it." The fox—Benjamin—wrung his paws. His ears were flat and his tail curled behind him, drawn in on himself. "We didn't need the money that badly—do people do that often?"

The descent and abrupt return from his monologue caught Aziz off guard. "Do people do what?"

"Sell cameras with the tapes still in them. Do people buy them?" He gestured to the section of video cameras. "If I buy one of those and it has a tape in it, do I get the tape too?"

"When we take an item, we take it as it is." Aziz kept his professional demeanor up. "And when a customer buys it, they buy it as it is."

Benjamin's ears stayed down. He glanced at the computer. "So…can you check? Can you see if someone bought it, or if you still have it?"

"Do you see it on the shelf?" Aziz didn't have to check the computer. No fox had brought in a video camera in the last two years, not to this store, anyway. Possibly on one of the days he hadn't been here, but those were few; possibly Benjamin had the location wrong and his—husband—had gone to one of Aziz's other locations. For that he could just text Naseeb, who worked at the store closest to this one.

Benjamin trudged over to the shelf to look. The marriage certificate remained on the counter, open but bowing up along the fold. It remained crisp, so it had likely been put away somewhere and well cared for. Likely by the fox, not by his—his husband, technically.

The paper drew Aziz's eyes again, and now he saw the species below the names. Benjamin Tonnen, red fox, and Gerald DeRoot—cougar.

Oh. And now he remembered the fox saying that Gerald was a cougar and felt foolish for assuming he would have been a fox. Regardless, that changed everything. He knew which camera it was now. And he remembered the cougar, too, large and sullen, in a stained white t-shirt and camo pants. He'd sold the camera along with an old VCR and a sewing machine, and he'd spoken barely a word. Aziz had given him the price and he hadn't complained nor tried to haggle, just put his large tan paw out and taken the cash. Off to buy alcohol, Aziz had thought, and he'd tagged the items and put them on the shelf.

The fox came back shaking his head. "There's one that's the same model, I think, but there's no tape in it."

"I am sorry," Aziz said. "I moved some cameras to one of my other locations because we had too many here. I will have it sent over if it is still there. The price should be the same as it is there on the shelf; fifty dollars, is it?"

He waited for Benjamin to haggle, to tell him that the camera hadn't been sold in a year and had been moved to another store where it still hadn't been sold (if it hadn't been sold), to offer him a small amount for the tape without the camera, but the fox perked his ears and only said, "Yes, that's fine. Which location? I could go now."

Aziz indicated the computer. "I will have to see if it is still there. I would hate for you to travel all the way to Cape Red for nothing."

Benjamin's ears flattened again. Cape Red was a wonderful place for a pawnshop, but not so much for casual visiting, and it would be an hour away by public transportation. "I don't really mind," he said.

"My store manager comes in every night anyway. I'll call and have her bring the camera. If it is still there." Aziz smiled. "And you can come back tomorrow and have it."

"Well…" Benjamin's claws tapped the counter glass, which there was a sign asking people not to do, but Aziz let it pass. "Can you call him right now? I'd hate for someone to walk in and buy it."

"Of course." Aziz smiled and picked up the phone.

The manager at the Cape Red store was a young hyena named Jennifer, bright and energetic. Aziz described the camera and the tape, and she put him on hold while she went to check her shelves. A moment later she came back, slightly breathless, and reported that she'd found a camera of that model with a tape in it. He instructed her to put it behind the counter and bring it in that evening.

"They still have it," he told Benjamin, who clearly had heard his conversation. His ears were up and he was smiling, his tail swishing behind him. "Video cameras don't sell so much anymore. One year is not unusual. Still, sometimes people want them."

"I know it's weird," the fox said. "A year later. I knew he'd sold the camera, but I was looking for the tape and I found the box but the tape wasn't in it. And I asked him and…" And there his ears went to the side and his eyes went down. "Anyway, I figured it was in the camera, because the last time I remembered us using it was…that tape was in it."

The cheetah nodded. "Is there anything else I can help you with?"

"Oh, no. So…tomorrow, I can come back…?"

"I should have it first thing."

"Thank you so much." Benjamin was all joy again, relief in his amber eyes, his ears upright and tail even wagging. "God, I'd hate to lose that tape. You know, we can buy another camera, but we can't make those memories over again, right?"

Aziz allowed the fox's delight to bring a smile to his muzzle as well. "I'm very glad we still have it. I'll look for you tomorrow morning."

"Yes, yes!" And the fox reached over and seized Aziz's paw, shook it vigorously, and then hurried out of the shop.

The cheetah held his paw and watched through the window as the fox stopped on the pavement in front of the store and then lost himself in the crowd of people going by. It was nice to be able to make someone happy in this business, he thought. He was about to return to his samovar when the crowd thinned for a moment. Through the gap in the flow of t-shirts, skirts, and tails, the figure of Benjamin was visible doubled over against the charcoal-grey lamppost. The fox's paws covered his face and he appeared to be shaking.

Was he sick? Aziz started around the counter, but a moment later, the fox straightened and rubbed his paws across his eyes. They left wet streaks that Aziz could see even through the glass. Naked emotion wrinkled the russet fur around the eyes and the white fur on his muzzle as Benjamin rubbed again, visibly composing himself. A moment later, a herd of deer in identical business suits crowded past the store window, and when they'd passed, Benjamin was gone.

Chapter Two: Doug

At five Aziz closed the store with the "back in 15 minutes" sign, retreated to the back for the *asr* prayer, letting go of his troubles. He focused on Allah and spoke the words glorifying Him. As he went through the ritual motions and spoke the familiar words, he felt the warmth of Allah's presence; not as strongly as when he would join his neighborhood mosque for the *isha* night prayer, but still present as He always was. He ended the prayer with the recital to his left and right, to the angel on his right that recorded all his good deeds and the angel on the left that recorded all his bad.

The shop saw a stream of customers from when he reopened until about seven, when people went to restaurants for dinner. He closed again for the sunset prayer, then stayed open until 7:45, when he closed his register and tidied up the store. His hours said until 8, and in the first few years of owning the store, he had made a point to stay until eight o'clock exactly. In recent years, as the neighborhood shifted and there were fewer people out late at night looking for bargains in discarded memories, he had become a little more lax. Tonight he left at five to eight and arrived at the café Casablanca at five after.

The main advantage of the café, Aziz and his friend Doug had decided, was that it sat directly below the large billboard atop the corner building, so it was the only place within a two-block square where a couple old friends could sit outside and not have to stare at whatever was being advertised this month. Last week the billboard had changed to an ad for *Space Wolf*, a movie made from a cartoon that had run twenty years ago. Aziz remembered Marquize loving the cartoon, but the movie was made using photorealistic characters rather than the charmingly drawn animation, and anyway he didn't want to think about his son.

Doug wasn't there yet, so Aziz got a table and a small coffee and waited for the Prevost's squirrel to arrive. As he leaned back in the metal frame chair, letting his tail swing free, the cheetah scanned the coffee shop. Many of the customers he recognized, a few from his mosque, but a large part of the clientele changed from day to day. Two of the regulars were a pair of wolves, another two a dingo and an arctic fox, both gay couples. The wolves were demonstrative and had kissed in public from almost the first time he'd seen them, but the dingo and fox were shyer. It was only a few years ago that Aziz had watched them more closely and had seen the signs of a bond there.

Tonight they sat over a pot of tea, smiling at a phone on the table. He wondered if they were texting to a mutual friend, or maybe looking at a photo album, or planning a trip together. Did Benjamin and his husband talk like that? In his experience, when one member of a couple sold a treasured possession, the pair was having problems. Might not even be together anymore. It was strange; though same-sex couples had been a part of the world around him for years, he'd never taken the time to imagine that their relationships might follow the same arcs as traditional marriages. Where he came from, husbands and wives didn't touch in public; even though here the customs were different, he had always viewed public displays of affection as sexual, and that was the only way he'd known same-sex couples to this point. Between that and searching on the Internet a few years ago, he had concluded that their pairings were mainly sexual arrangements.

"Zeez?"

Aziz had been staring at the fox and dingo for who knows how long. He hid his discomfort and looked up at Doug with a smile. "Evening, Doug."

"Lost in thought?"

"Something like that. We got the offer letter from Vorvarts today."

"Finally. Was it what you expected?" Doug dropped his bulk into the chair opposite Aziz and straightened his t-shirt over reddish arm and chest fur.

"About."

"And?"

Aziz looked deliberately away from the dingo and fox. From here he could not see the Homeporium, only rows of old brownstones. Were it not for the strain in his back and the aches that traveled around his joints, he could almost believe he was sitting here twenty years earlier. "I have to talk to Halifa before we go to the meeting. It's difficult. I don't want to leave this area. Halifa says the area is leaving us."

"You're telling me. I had three different people come in today looking for the Morey Tanderson book. Fortunately I also read that article in the Port City Review and had stocked a few dozen of them." He leaned in. "It's a terrible book, so self-indulgent. I knew all the millennials would want it."

In general, the ages of the Homeporium residents fell onto a neat bell curve centered around thirty, but to Doug, a "millennial" was anyone under forty. Aziz smiled slightly. "Did you read it?"

"I had to. People ask me about it." The squirrel shook his black-furred head. "The things I do for my job."

"I had a customer come in looking for an item his husband had pawned." Aziz forced himself to say 'husband' and was pleased at how natural it sounded.

"Ah." Doug signaled the waiter. "Familiar story."

"With a twist." He turned his head casually back toward the dingo and fox, who were now talking, the phone still on the table between them. Aziz leaned forward to pick up his tea and stopped. Behind the dingo and fox, a cougar sat alone in a tight-fitting olive green t-shirt, his feet framing an Army duffel bag below the table. One paw held an iced tea, the other his phone, which he stared intently at.

The memory was a year old, but could that be Gerald? Aziz narrowed his eyes, trying to see around the dingo, but at that moment the waiter filled his view.

They ordered their simple dinner, and Doug ordered a chamomile tea. "So that's why you were looking at Michael and Panno."

"You know their names?" Aziz's ears perked up.

"I met them a few months ago in the bookstore. They were looking for science fiction, so I gave them *Dog Country* and they came back to tell me they'd enjoyed it." He tilted his head, looking at Aziz. "They're nice. I can introduce you if you like."

"That's okay," Aziz said quickly.

Doug shook his head. "Have it your way."

"It's not…" The cheetah sighed. "Let's talk about something else."

"My friend." Doug reached across and rested a paw on Aziz's. The touch was familiar and friendly, not intimate, but Aziz couldn't help flicking his eyes over to the fox and dingo, who were also—no; they were holding paws in an intimate manner, the dingo's thumb rubbing over the fox's white fur. He snapped his eyes back to Doug as the squirrel went on. "The past is receding very quickly. The future encroaches on us everywhere."

Aziz chose to believe that Doug was starting a new conversation, not talking about his relationship with gay people still. "Have you signed your offer yet?"

Doug shook his head. "Waiting for the meeting. But I'll send it off right after that. Did you see the implicit threat?"

"Implicit threat?"

"The expiration date. After which they'll come after us."

Years earlier, when planning the Homeporium, Vorvarts had run into one obstinate homeowner, a pine marten who had been attached to her brownstone and refused to sell. They had sent inspectors around to find housing code violations, had hired lawyers to scrutinize her tax records, and had eventually harassed her—completely legally—into giving up her home for a third of what they'd originally offered. "Halifa worries about that too, but our records are in order. I don't believe they will go to those lengths if several of us hold out. Giverny said he expects they might increase their offer."

Giverny was the lawyer they and Doug had both used. "Or…"

"There is always that chance. Halifa and I will discuss it." Aziz exhaled. "There is the neighborhood, too. The mosque, the apartments down the street…if they take over here, how long before the rents rise and those people must leave?"

"And that'll be good for your business for a while longer."

Aziz inclined his head. "I hate to look at it that way, but it is business. I can't stop the neighborhood from changing."

Doug laughed and cut him off. "I'm sure Tanska will have something to say about that."

"I think we can survive here a little longer, even if they build around us." Aziz sipped his tea, thinking about the fiery Siberian tiger. "It would be nice if we'd been able to convince Polavic and Jenella not to sell."

"You think Halifa would want to stay if you could have a solid half-block?"

"No." Aziz rubbed the side of his muzzle. "But the situation would be different. She would understand that."

The squirrel leaned across the table, close to Aziz. His broad, pudgy shoulders strained at the thin yellow polo shirt. "And if Tanska agrees to sell…would you also?"

"There would be little point in staying then." The cheetah pressed his paws together. "But I still wouldn't know what I could do after selling."

"Besides run your other stores?"

Aziz had spent time at the other stores when setting them up, but now only traveled to them two or three times a year, while Halifa managed most of the finances. They were foreign nations to him, albeit ones that paid him monthly. "They run themselves."

"You'd have enough money to do almost anything you want." Doug looked up at the cheetah. "Travel, give up work, help people here or in your home country."

"That's the problem." Aziz rubbed his muzzle. "I'm not sure what I want. What are you going to do?"

"My son wants me to move out to Coronado with him. I would like to see a little more of the world. I could do both those things and more if I only had the time."

"And that makes it difficult."

Doug smiled. "May we all have such problems."

Chapter Three: The Tape

After the meal, Aziz walked the three blocks to the Devos Musjid Al-Islam, a small brick building that looked like any other storefront, large window giving out onto the street with a green awning where two ground squirrels and an ibex sheltered from the evening heat, sharing a bowl of fresh dates likely from the grocery next door. They waved as he passed and asked about his day; he made small talk and accepted a date, the sweetness bursting in his mouth as he went inside.

Halifa preferred to pray at home. Aziz suspected that in recent years her sense of community had been broken. And even though he rarely lingered long after prayer, he did love the feeling of being surrounded by others at the night and morning prayers.

Brushing aside the privacy curtain, he entered the spacious prayer room and crossed to the males' side where he greeted a red fox, a pair of mice, and a pangolin who had been at the café. It was comforting simply to stand among them as they talked, leaning against one corkboard wall that held community announcements, waiting for the imam to lead them in prayer. And kneeling, prostrating himself as he spoke his prayer with a dozen others, he felt closer to his god, his fellows, his world.

Lately, that feeling hadn't lasted much beyond the prayer itself. Over the last six months, most of the post-prayer conversation in the mosque had been around the changing neighborhood. Thus far, the mosque was not in the sphere of Vorvarts, but that sphere was expanding. Rents had jumped, nearly doubled in the last five years, and people feared what a new development would bring. "They couldn't get us out by calling us terrorists," went the oft-repeated line, "so they're trying to drive us out with money."

Aziz knew that there was no sinister government conspiracy, merely capitalism and opportunity at work, and that all religions in Upper Devos were being affected more or less equally. Though he shared their worries about the neighborhood, he stood to profit from its development as the mosque's only business owner on Nassau Street, so he had politely excluded himself from those conversations. The problem was that that only left matters of faith, local sports, or his family as topics of conversation. That last had not been a good topic for three years, and Aziz did not follow sports, and these days the matters of faith all seemed tied into the fate of the Muslim community. So Aziz stayed a short time out of courtesy and then excused himself, walking out and down through the humid, dark evening back to his store.

Jennifer lived near Aziz and Halifa, so she often dropped by the store late at night and sometimes stayed to talk to Aziz when he came back to do the cash accounting. Tonight, though, she'd simply left the camera on the counter with a note saying that she had a date and had to leave, and she hoped this was the right camera.

It took him only twenty minutes to do the accounting, and like most evenings, the numbers lined up into orderly columns and matched the cash in the till to a degree that reassured him that the world was an orderly place. He liked the feel of cash in his paws, and even credit card receipts felt more solid than the numbers that appeared from his online storefront. Much as he preferred to look his customers in the eye, the online sales had kept his stores afloat when many other pawnshops had failed. The uneasiness of dealing with people he couldn't see was outweighed by the weekly income they brought in.

Once he'd finished, he picked up the camera. Heavier than he'd anticipated, even for as large as it was, nearly the size of his head. Probably about five years old. He opened it and looked at the unlabeled tape inside. Nothing there to show whose it was. He should probably play it so he could confirm that the tape was Ben's. It wasn't any more intrusive than anything else he'd done over twenty years of taking other people's possessions. He'd gotten nude pictures out of books where they'd been shoved and forgotten, old letters in pockets of briefcases, countless photos and video on cameras either forgotten or ignored. Sometimes he looked through them to see what kind of person had pawned their camera; often the original owner had passed on or moved out and the camera held a surprising array of images compared to the person who'd brought it in. Once Aziz had found photos of white powder, needles, and piles of bank notes. That he'd reported to the police. The rest he kept to himself.

Jennifer hadn't brought any cables with the camera, but he had a few with other cameras, so he walked over to his shelf where seven blank television screens waited silently. Aziz plugged the cables into one of the TVs at his eye level and stepped back, holding the camera. Eyes fixed on the screen, he pressed Play.

For a moment the only sound was the whirr of the camera spinning the tape. Then static appeared on the TV, crackling, and an image burst onto the screen: golden-white sand and turquoise water and the froth of

waves. A moment later a cougar in a tight swimsuit ran into the frame, laughing and waving. "Put the camera down!" he yelled. "Come on, let's swim!"

Muscles around his dense body spoke to youth or a good workout regimen or both, and the swimsuit was very tight indeed. Gerald moved with a weight and force that no cheetah in Aziz's experience did, but with a common feline suppleness. Aziz looked closer, only to see if he could identify this cougar as the one from the coffee shop. It was hard to tell when one was nearly naked and bursting with joy while the other had been clothed and devoid of any emotion, but the build was the same, at least. His wide, happy eyes glowed green through a brown filter: a soft hazel color. Aziz searched for another distinguishing mark and then leaned back, disgusted at his own invasive curiosity.

"In a minute," a louder voice called from off screen. The image wobbled, then steadied, and then a fox's black paw waved in front of the camera. "Looks good," he said. A moment later the fox himself, light red fur glowing in the sun, sprinted down the beach toward the waves, red tail streaming out behind him with its bright white tip overexposed. For a moment, Aziz thought the fox wasn't wearing any clothes, and then he turned and the bright red Speedo flashed into view.

In the short glimpse he had in the faraway picture, Aziz couldn't say for sure whether the happy fox on the beach was the same as the desperate fox who'd begged him to get the camera back. And the scene intrigued him. He and Halifa had gone to the beach, but only the local one here, back when their son Marquize was young. They'd let him ride some of the smaller rides on the boardwalk, had bought him a treat of fried dough and powdered sugar that had ended up all over his paws and muzzle, and had splashed around in the tame waves. Coming from an inland desert city, the ocean was a novelty, but one that made Aziz uneasy at first, both from the wide expanse of water and from the state of undress of the people enjoying it. Their son had loved it, and Halifa had enjoyed the cool water, so they went two or three times every summer until Marquize went away to boarding school. Aziz hadn't realized that he missed it until this moment.

That beach had been crowded with people; they'd had to arrive before nine in the morning to be sure of finding a spot. The beach in the video here was empty save for the fox and cougar. Was it a private beach? Hard to imagine they could afford to vacation on a private beach and then a few years later have to pawn the camera they'd used to record it. Not unusual, of course; people lost their jobs every day. Maybe the cougar had been military and something had happened to him.

"Come back!" the fox yelled down the beach, and the cougar hesitated, his feet already splashing in the waves, then ran back up. Sand stuck to his fur as he ran, and then he got close enough to sling an arm around the fox's shoulders and his sandy feet were out of the frame.

"What? I wanna swim."

The fox pointed to the camera, and now Aziz saw for certain that he was Benjamin. "Kiss me, husband," he said, and the weight he gave to that word made it sound as shiny and new as it must have been to them then.

It brought a sparkle to the cougar's eyes. He wrapped his paw around the fox's shoulder and bent down to kiss him, the two of them pressing closer and closer.

Aziz shut off the tape. Even as he replaced it in the camera, though, the image of the couple embracing stuck with him, and that caused his tail to twitch and his head to turn, ears perked, though there was nobody else in the shop and nobody could see in with the grating down over the front windows. Spying on others was a sin, but as the owner of a pawnshop, he had long ago made his peace with the brief glimpses of others' lives that passed through his paws every day. Early on, he had sometimes tried to discover more, and each time had reproved himself and added a *du'a* asking forgiveness to his prayers that evening.

Now that curiosity resurfaced. What was it that made this tape so important to Benjamin? Was it simply that this was a memory of a happier time?

Aziz and Halifa had once been that close, though they'd never taken such pure delight in each other's company. They had clung together out of shared past and emotional connection, out of having escaped the destitution of their home to make a better life for their son. In those days, they had been full of accomplishment, equal partners in their business and family. Halifa had delighted in the freedom she was afforded here, where perhaps real estate agents would give her a second look but would not speak over her to her husband or forbid her from signing documents. And Marquize had blossomed in the new world, making friends easily. If he'd resisted some of the duties of Islam, Aziz and Halifa hadn't had the heart to punish him too severely. Children rebelled against their parents and found their own paths, and those paths would lead them back. Or should. And always in the back of their minds was the cub who should have been Marquize's sister, stillborn, a message perhaps to remind them of how valuable Marquize himself was. And yet that permissiveness had led to…

Aziz forced his thoughts back to the dingo and arctic fox in the café, to the pair of wolves there. Their lives and stories seemed to open up to him, as though he'd been looking at a pane of glass edge-on and upon stepping to the side had noticed a design etched on it. But he couldn't yet see what that design was. If he could see it, would it help him understand his own life? Would it help him understand his son?

On his desk, sitting in a back corner, there was a small bottle of rosewater. Dust stuck to his fingers as he picked it up and turned it over, the delicate scent tickling his nostrils. Halifa used to like when he wore rosewater. He opened the bottle and the scent grew stronger; he turned it over into his paw pad and dabbed at the white fur below his chin, then stoppered the bottle and put it back.

Chapter Four: Halifa

He walked home through the muggy evening and even opened his shirt to the air. A wolf in a skirt turned her—his?—nose as Aziz walked by, no doubt intrigued by the rose scent around the cheetah. An Anglic polecat named Maggie waved as he passed her, and he waved back. He might not know all the people specifically, but he knew many of them. And yet he hadn't seen Benjamin before, and Gerald only the one time that he could recall. Unless the cougar had been at the café and Aziz hadn't noticed him. That idea bothered him more than it should; he couldn't know everyone, could he?

Out of habit, he checked his shop as he walked by, but everything seemed to be in order. At the corner, Tanska was closing up the pastry store, and Aziz thought that talking about the Vorvarts offer with the tiger might distract him from thinking about the tape. So he waited five minutes, after which she saw him and raised a paw with two fingers: two minutes. He nodded and leaned against the glass, smiling hello to the polar bear couple who'd bought their first electric guitars from him years before and who still dropped off flyers for their performances whenever they had one.

The door to the store clicked open and Tanska came out, dressed in tight jeans and a halter top. She held out a napkin to Aziz. "It's good to see you," she said with a smile, and turned to lock the door.

"Thank you," he said, and unfolded the napkin to reveal a pair of flat biscuits. He brought them to his nose, sniffing the sweet, spicy ginger, and then rewrapped them. "I'll bring one to Halifa."

"I guess you got the letter today as well." Tanska slipped the keys into her pocket and looked across the street at the Homeporium. "Assholes."

"It's a lot of money."

"Don't tell me you're thinking about selling. I'll take those biscuits right back." She swiped a paw at him jokingly.

He sighed and shook his head. "But Halifa was willing to sell for two thirds of what they're offering. When she sees the letter…"

"We need to hold out, Zeez. As long as we can." She didn't have to look across the street again to remind him what was at stake.

The cheetah's tail lashed; he made an effort to still it. "I want to, believe me. I love the store, the street. But I don't think we will convince anyone else to stay."

The tiger rubbed her paws together. "You smell like rosewater."

"I know."

She stepped out onto the sidewalk, and Aziz fell in beside her. They lived in the same direction for at least two blocks. "I'm sorry. I see all this happening in front of me. I'm going to lose my store because everyone here is tired of fighting. They're going to give up, cash in, and that cancer," she swept her paw toward the blue glass as they left it behind, "will keep spreading."

"You aren't losing the store. What they offered us is enough to start up again somewhere else."

Tanska reached down around an oblivious raccoon couple to pick up a discarded can, and carried it to the recycling bin on the street corner. "You have other locations. It's easy for you. Easier," she amended. "Look at me. I have no husband, no children, nothing but the store. I'm forty-one. I'm too old to start over."

"I'm nearly forty-six," Aziz said lightly.

Tanska shook her head. "You have a wife. You have a—another store."

"I have memories here, friends like you."

The tiger's head lifted as they walked on and the Homeporium passed from view. "You don't think that keeping this is worth fighting for? You think those people know each other the way we do? They don't want a neighborhood; they want a mall. They want convenience and proximity to the city, not a community. You know how many of them have joined the neighborhood association since that went up?"

Aziz did, but he let her tell him. She held up her thumb and forefinger in a circle. "None."

"Maybe they didn't feel welcome."

"We put flyers up." She shook her head. "They don't care. They don't want to be part of an association. They're happy to pay someone else to do it." Now with the same paw, she rubbed the thumb and forefinger against each other. "Money. They got it, so they don't need people. And that's what Vorvarts is counting on. Yes, it's a lot of money. But then what would I do?"

"Take that cruise finally? Meet a nice tiger on the beach?" Aziz cursed his tongue, then realized that Tanska would have no idea why that meant something to him at this moment. "You could invest in another bakery?"

"If I haven't met someone by now…" Tanska left the actual gender of her desires as vague as always. "I suppose I could look for another bakery in another neighborhood, help them out. But then what? In five years, another Vorvarts comes calling and again I'm left with nothing but money. That's not what I want."

"Well, then." Aziz took a breath. "How would you convince the Association not to sell?"

"Ah ha!" She beamed at him. "Now you're talking. Let's come up with a strategy."

Aziz shook his head. "It's hard to fight against money. Some of them want to spend more time with their families. And it's hard to imagine when we'll get this kind of money again."

"What if we pooled our resources and advertised how old-school our neighborhood is? People love that nostalgia. Your shop is almost a museum, mine is a trip to Moskva…we could become a destination neighborhood."

"We were." Aziz walked by a hare who lived on their street and waved; the hare returned his wave with one paw, staring at a phone held in the other. "And people came to that destination, and decided they wanted a huge mall."

"They didn't decide that. Vorvarts decided it."

"The Homeporium voted in favor of the expansion."

Tanska huffed. "I don't know why people go out of their way to move to a neighborhood and then tear up the neighborhood once they're there. They didn't even come to any of the shops once that abomination went up."

"Some do."

She rounded on him. "Why are you being such wet snow? I thought we were on the same side."

"Wet snow?" He had to hide a smile.

"Tch. What do they say here? Wet…"

"Blanket?"

Her brow furrowed. "Maybe. But sometimes I feel like you'd be happier if you let Halifa sell the store. Then you wouldn't have to make a decision."

"It's not that." He sighed, unsure how to explain his feelings without hurting hers. "I want to be realistic about it. I don't want to sell, but…"

"I know what it is." They had reached the point where they would have to part. "You want to be on the winning side. And you don't think we can win."

"That is not true!"

"Which part?"

He looked back into her eyes. "I want us to stay," he said. "But I can't see any way to make anyone else stay. We spent thousands of dollars researching the community laws to see if we had legal grounds to prevent it. Fighting it in court would take hundreds of thousands, more than you and I have, and if we did that it would destroy the community anyway; the rest of the Association would hate us for delaying their payouts."

"They'd thank us when we save the street."

"But what if we lost?"

"If we put up the fight, they might think it wasn't worth the trouble and build somewhere else."

He gestured back to the blue glass towers. "Which of the other three neighboring streets? The block with the subway station and transit center? Or the ones facing the backs of their apartments? There's a park there and it starts running up against the town hall in that direction anyway."

She smacked her open paw into the post of the traffic light. "I told them. They said, 'oh, those buildings are eyesores, let's let them build there,' and I said 'don't let them in, they'll just want more.'"

Aziz stayed quiet at the unspoken reminder that he, too, had voted to let Vorvarts tear down the ugly yellow brick things. "It was those boutiques over on Rhys," he said. "All that Old World money came in, and people with money followed. We welcomed their money then; now they want to use it to change where they live. The time to stop this was six, eight years ago."

"I don't think it's too late. I'll think of something to do." She raised a paw. "Goodnight."

"Goodnight," he said, and watched as she walked away, his brow creased in worry. His resolve to stay felt weakest around Tanska's fiery idealism, because she always made him wonder, *is this how everyone else sees me?* Still, he couldn't abandon her. He'd known many people who undertook crusades, and when the crusade was over, they lost focus and direction in their life. If—when—they lost the current battle to Vorvarts, he didn't want that to happen to Tanska if he could at all avoid it.

الْوَقْتِ الَّذِيْ يُرِيْدُ

When he arrived home, Halifa was already in her room reading. Aziz hung his keys on the hook near the door, glanced around the dark living room and kitchen, and then walked up to the second floor. He knocked on the half-open door, then stepped inside from the dark hallway into the warm soft light.

His wife lay in her bed with a white satin nightdress on. As he entered, she set a bookmark into her book and placed it on the nightstand. "Good evening."

"I'm sorry I'm late." The beach, the fox and cougar, the tape flashed through his mind, but he kept his demeanor calm as he set the gingerbread biscuits and the couriered letter down on her nightstand. "I stopped to talk to Tanska."

Halifa picked up the letter first and scanned it for the sale amount. Her eyebrows rose slightly, and she refolded the letter and replaced it, taking one of the biscuits. "She won't sell."

"She doesn't want to." He took the other biscuit and leaned back against the wall, eating it slowly. Sweet ginger spice filled his mouth. "What do you think?"

She smiled. "You know what I think."

"And you know what I think."

"Yes." She finished her biscuit and licked her lips. "You are comfortable in this life we've built. Selling the store to you means we should also sell this house, and move...closer to one of the other stores? Take over one of them personally?" Her fingers tapped against each other. "If we came up with a plan, you would feel better about selling."

"Which you want to do," he countered, "because you feel that this store is going to decline and we would have to sell it soon anyway. You would rather spend time with your charities and move on from the business."

She inclined her head. "So where does that leave us?"

He brushed crumbs from his muzzle. "Are we too old to make a change?"

"No," Halifa said immediately. "We have lived one life, but we have time to live another one as well."

"Another life?" Aziz brought a paw to his muzzle. The rosewater filled his nostrils. "But where to start?"

She folded her paws over her stomach and smiled. "We didn't know where to start here twenty years ago, and yet we did."

"We had Ahmad and Zaynab." The lions who had welcomed them to Upper Devos had passed away seven and eight years previous. Both Aziz and Halifa bowed their heads for a moment. "And now who do we have?"

There was a time some years ago when she would have said, "We have our family." Now she said, "Why do we need someone else?"

He shook his head. "The meeting is tomorrow. We have to decide what we're doing by then."

"You know that the smart business decision is to sell. The money we would make by staying open in this location for another year or two, as people move out, would not come close to the price they've offered us." She softened her tone. "And you don't have to figure out what you want to do right away. We will have plenty of time."

When he didn't answer, she reached to the nightstand and picked up her phone. Her fingers tapped, chatting with friends, most likely. Aziz thought about the couple on the beach, how close they'd been. His gaze swept over the hardwood floor, the nightstand, the bed, and up to Halifa. "How was your day?"

She looked up from her phone and fixed him with a puzzled expression. "It was fine, thank you. How was yours?"

"The store was not terribly busy. You had a meeting with the...the Balanore Relief Fund?"

Slowly, she laid the phone down on the sheets next to her tail. Her puzzlement turned to amusement. "That was Thursday. Today was the Play Around committee meeting. And it went well. We're talking to builders about what we can put into the new playground over in Thornberry Street, and ..." She broke off and tilted her head, looking at him. "Are you interested because we might be selling the shop? Do you want to come to the next meeting? I would not recommend the Play Around committee, but the Balanore Relief, that one you might be interested in."

"No," he said. "Just wondering what you've been doing." But would he be interested in the charities? That might be an avenue he could follow, using his money and time to help others. He admired that about Halifa, and while these charities often seemed like crusades as well, there were enough of them for her to spread her energies and never acquire a fanatic's focus about any individual one. He had tried to involve himself with her charities years ago but had grown frustrated at the amount of paperwork and planning that went into it. More patient, Halifa enjoyed the time spent working with her friends in the charity groups, but Aziz didn't know any of those people. It felt to him as though the charity meetings had become more focused on social business than charity business, and that if someone had come up with a document that would solve their problem with a single signature, they would all have been disappointed because it would have meant an end to the meeting before they had a chance to go out for coffee together.

Still, if he didn't have his shop to manage, he might have the patience for it. With Halifa at his side, he could navigate those meetings, do some good for the world, bury himself in other people's problems.

The problems of Balanore, though, those were massive: a huge flood had devastated the area and thousands of people were without homes. And yet, Aziz would never have heard of the disaster if not for Halifa's involvement. She kept up on the news better than he did.

"There's always something to do," she said. "Always someone to take care of. Refugees in other countries, Muslims in this country, children everywhere. I showed you the school we built in Princeport?"

"Let me see it again." He leaned over as she called up pictures on her phone.

The school, a low building with prefab walls and roof, gleamed with recent rain. Next to it stood a small group of mice, hutia, ocelots, and a few other species, their fur soaked but their smiles wide. "If we had more time," Halifa said, "we could actually go to some of these sites and meet these people. It would be nice to be more directly involved."

Aziz could think of little he'd want less than to get his fur soaked in the warm, humid air of some devastated region. Yes, they would be doing good work, but there were other ways to do it. "It sounds great," he nodded, and looked through the rest of the photos with interest, albeit detached interest.

"And here," she said, bringing up one last album, "is a shelter for runaway teens."

The unassuming house looked to be located in a poorer Port City neighborhood. Aziz was about to ask where it was when he noticed the rainbow flag sticker, prominent in a front window. He cleared his throat. "What kind of teens?"

"Well," Halifa said, "most of them left their families because their families didn't approve of their lifestyle."

"I see." He stood. "Thank you for showing me."

She followed him with her eyes, but didn't say anything as he left her room.

Their townhouse had three stories, but both his and Halifa's rooms were on the second story. Upstairs was storage and their son's room, barely used for the last seven years and not at all for the last three. Aziz padded over the familiar intricate designs of the plush hallway carpet, one paw on the thick wooden railing by the stair. On that peacock design his son had sat holding the knee he'd banged into the doorway after running too fast up and down the stairs; on that Tree of Life Aziz had stood with the papers for their second store and read the terms to Halifa, with Marquize dancing around their legs in contagious excitement; that patch of carpet on the stairs was worn where Marquize had always stepped to the left, taking the stairs hastily even into his teen years; the stair above it was almost new because he had always leapt up that stair as though it was bad luck to touch it. On the stair above that one, Marquize had stood sullenly and listened to Aziz lecture him, then had turned and walked up to his room without another word.

Here, on this row of diamonds, Aziz had stood and watched his son walk down the stairs and out of his house for the last time. Of course he would remember that now, after Halifa had so indelicately reminded him of it. He turned to the door of his room and walked inside.

He often indulged himself in memories before retiring, but tonight he put them out of his head and knelt on the prayer rug, already oriented properly, and give himself to the *isha*, the night-time prayer. When he'd completed that, he felt calmer and more sure of his place in the world, and he stood and stretched, walking over to sit at his desk.

This room had formerly been Aziz's office. His desk had been below the window that looked out onto the window of the Jacksons' brownstone; now it was in the far corner so that there was room for his bed and wardrobe. He could no longer remember when the bed had been acquired nor even who had acquired it. He and Halifa had agreed one day that the bed they shared was too small for them both, and that the best solution was to buy a new bed for his office.

He only sat long enough to make sure that no urgent messages had come in over e-mail, and then he undressed and lay back in his bed. Usually following the night prayer, his mind was clear and he could think about his schedule and duties the following day. Tonight, however, his thoughts remained a jumble of the offer letter, the tape, the talk with Tanska, the school in Princeport. Rosewater remained strong in his nose, reminding him of his transgression even though he'd already told himself there was nothing wrong with it. Finally, he accepted that sleep would not come unless he relaxed, and he padded to the bathroom.

Halifa knocked while he was waiting for the shower to heat up. "Aziz? Is everything okay?"

"I spilled rosewater on myself at the office," he said. "It's keeping me from sleeping."

She didn't respond for a moment, then said, "All right," and moved away from the door.

Aziz washed himself clean, and whether it was the absence of rosewater or the warm shower, when he returned to his bed, he closed his eyes and fell asleep without any more trouble.

Chapter Five: Delivery

In the morning, he set the camera on the counter by the cash register with a neat price tag reading "$50" and another saying, "SOLD."

Aziz believed that if he got one customer in the first half hour, it would be a good day. This belief had sometimes been proven wrong, but by and large it had held true enough that he watched the clock tick toward 9:30 with anxiety until that first customer entered the store. Even someone selling rather than buying was good luck, though the sellers rarely came in so early.

Today, his coffee from café Casablanca had barely cooled when the front door bell tinkled, and Benjamin walked in, tugging nervously at the collar of his green shirt, a blue tie swinging above khaki pants. He walked right up to the counter, eyes on Aziz. "Hi," he said. "I'm sorry if—oh."

Aziz slid the camera to the middle of the counter, drawing the fox's eyes to it. For a moment, he found it difficult to talk, contrasting the love in the eyes of the fox on the tape with the desperation in the eyes of the fox at his counter. He shook his head clear and focused on the camera. "I believe it is the right camera. If you want to check the tape, ah…" There was no reason he shouldn't suggest this, not if he hadn't seen the tape. "I can hook up one of the televisions."

"Ah, no." Benjamin grabbed the camera and turned it over, then ejected the tape and stared at it. His ears came up and he looked like he might cry again. "This…this is it," he managed, and pushed the tape back in. "You said fifty?"

Aziz indicated the small sign. "Of course," Benjamin said, holding the camera in one paw while fumbling for his wallet with the other. "Thank you. Thank you so much. You have no idea what this means."

"You're most welcome." Aziz took the proffered credit card and ran it, then presented the fox with a receipt to sign. Benjamin held onto the camera while signing and then pushed the receipt back. The passion and devotion was as evident on his muzzle now as it had been in the tape, and again Aziz felt curiosity and shame at his spying burn together in his chest.

Benjamin hurried out without another word. Aziz followed him with his eyes, but the fox didn't break down against the post and cry again, simply took off into the crowd and vanished with a flick of his white-tipped red tail.

Aziz's own tail curled behind him, and for the rest of the day he kept seeing the fox's bright smile and perked ears. To have seen that kind of passion up close—and for another male, no less—kept him on edge, as though he'd looked out to see that the Homeporium's glass had turned a hazel green. Even his midday and sunset prayers didn't settle him as they normally would. Finally he closed the store early again and headed for the café, hoping a talk with Doug would keep his mind off it.

But before the Prevost's squirrel had even arrived, Aziz spotted the cougar in military gear again. He sat by himself at a table, one large paw (with a gold band on the ring finger) wrapped around a tall glass, the other resting on a tablet computer that held most of his attention. Aziz saw again that body in the tight swimsuit and closed his eyes until the reality of the café reasserted itself and he could study Gerald again.

He was as certain as he could be that this was Benjamin's (ex?) husband. The cougar's muzzle had a similar marking and his eyes were the same warm hazel. His t-shirt was not a uniform olive green, on reflection. Discolored patches that appeared to be food or drink stains marred the area below the chest. As Aziz watched, Gerald gulped down the last of his iced tea, wiped his mouth with the back of his paw, then wiped the paw on his shirt as he got up from the table, eyes still glued to his tablet. Those eyes…Aziz couldn't look away. They'd been so alive on the tape, and now they seemed dead. Had Benjamin messaged his husband to let him know he'd gotten the tape back? Was that the message Gerald was looking at so disinterestedly? What had gone wrong between them?

If Doug had shown up at that moment, Aziz might not have stood and excused himself to the waiter who had come over to take his order. He might have watched Gerald's black-tipped tail flicking as the cougar walked out of the patio and onto the sidewalk, disappearing into the busy crowd as his husband had earlier that morning, and then put Gerald out of his mind as he talked to Doug. But Doug was a few minutes late that day, and by the time he would arrive, Aziz was already turning the corner behind Gerald a block away.

The cheetah slid easily through the crowd, asking himself as he did what exactly he thought he was going to do. Follow Gerald home? This was spying, far beyond whatever he had done by looking at their tape in the pawnshop. *If you already know you will be asking forgiveness for an act, should you not cease doing it?* Yes, of course he should. He stopped and raised his nose to the sky. *But what if I could make a difference in their lives? What if I could give them advice? What if I'm meant to give them advice?*

Benjamin had shared part of his life with Aziz. He'd been so desperate to recover the camera that if Aziz hadn't seen Gerald that day, he might've thought Benjamin was grieving his husband's death. So maybe they were separated. But Benjamin had shown how much he still loved his husband, and maybe, Aziz thought, maybe Gerald needed to hear that from a third party.

So he would talk to Gerald, and he would only follow him until he found a convenient place to talk, somewhere the cougar would be after Aziz's evening prayer. Then it would not be so bad, following him. He would still have to ask forgiveness, but at least he would have made something positive out of his actions.

Gerald and his swinging tail made their way toward Larchmont, and for a moment Aziz thought he might be going to the address on Benjamin's license. That would be a good sign and then he would not even have to talk to Gerald. But the cougar strode across Larchmont, past the quiet street of row house apartments and small community gardens, down past the small local branch of the bank and its glowing ATM, past the liquor store with the cacomistle in the hoodie slouched out front who reeked of rum. This was only six blocks from Aziz's store, but in the opposite direction from his home, and a neighborhood he didn't know well; still Upper Devos, but shading into Cottage Hill. Across from the liquor store was a small tea shop that smelled of pastries and herbal tea, where a matronly llama fed crumbs to a parrot perched on her arm. She seemed oblivious to the drunk cacomistle, and he to her, and the people walking by on the sidewalks—foxes, wolves, deer, rats, raccoons— ignored both the figures.

The cougar, too, made his way through the neighborhood with confidence and purpose. He paused at the corner in front of a fur trimming salon, and Aziz hung back so as not to be too obviously following him. When the light changed, the cheetah crossed at the rear of the crowd, with Gerald at the front, but he was tall enough to keep his target in view as the cougar walked past a deli and ducked into a bar. Aziz stopped and looked up at the bar's sign: "Founder's."

He made a note of the streets and then hurried back the way he'd come, back past the shop to Devos Musjid Al-Islam, arriving just in time to wash and kneel for the evening prayer. But even though he recited the words with everyone else, his mind found it difficult to surrender himself to Allah. At times in the past he had been preoccupied, but only once, during those terrible days when he and Marquize had been fighting, had he been so distracted that even the prayer didn't bring him solace. At that time, he'd taken comfort in the existence of a higher power who would watch over him, in the benefit that came from obeying Allah's orders to pray regularly. The company of all the others around him had comforted him: here were people with their own lives and problems, and yet they all came together in these prayers.

Now he could not wrench his mind away from the fox and cougar, either the happy couple years in the past or the troubled couple of today. And why not? He and Halifa had maintained their marriage without passion for years; they had survived the betrayal of their son, where Aziz had seen such problems tear other marriages apart. Or was he trying to understand Marquize himself, that adorable little cub who had turned into a withdrawn teen and not only cut himself off from Islam by having sex with males, but repudiated his parents' faith by proclaiming his homosexuality to their faces?

Aziz's paws shook; here, finally, was a thought that could drive Benjamin and Gerald from his mind. It had been three years since he'd spoken to Marquize, three years since his son had moved to the other side of the country to live with his lover. And here Aziz was, chasing after another homosexual couple to help them get back together? If he did, though, that would prove that he wasn't those names Marquize had shouted at him, that he was merely devoted to his faith. Homosexuality was...was fine, if your religion permitted it. His did not.

Not that he would call Marquize and tell him. But he would know in his heart that he was following Allah's guidance, and that included reaching out to people in need, even if they drank alcohol, ate pork, or took lovers of the same gender. He spoke a short *du'a* asking for forgiveness for the manner in which he had determined a place to talk to Gerald. And thus relieved, Aziz rose from his prayer.

Chapter Six: Tanska

This evening, he didn't wait to make conversation with anyone at the mosque, but hurried out the door. He had gotten two blocks before his phone's alarm chimed. He looked down and saw a reminder for the Merchants Association meeting.

He'd completely forgotten that that was tonight. The alarm continued to flash on his phone while he weighed it in one palm. He couldn't skip the meeting, even if he had been completely in agreement with Halifa about how to vote. Gerald would have to wait until after the meeting, or maybe tomorrow night, and if he weren't at Founders still, Aziz would talk to him the next time he saw the cougar at the café, no matter how many of his friends and acquaintances might see them. He'd promised to do that and now was obliged.

The Merchants Association met in a classroom of the local elementary school, which Marquize had never attended; Aziz and Halifa had sent him to a private school, and when he'd shown more aptitude for tennis than anything else, they'd sent him down to a school in Pensa. Aziz knew this room more as a meeting space than a classroom, stuffy on summer evenings and chilly on winter nights, the decorations changing from month to month as the cubs practiced their letters and drew holiday pictures. Tonight, with school out of session, the drawings were about what each cub's family would do during the summer break: pictures of beaches and forests, one of Lutèce's iconic Koechlin Tower.

All seventeen of the members of the Association had said they would be present tonight, some with their families, so the room was more crowded than he was used to. Doug waved to him from near the back, but he'd only taken two steps toward the squirrel when he saw Halifa at the front of the room, focused on her phone in the pre-meeting chaos that raged around her. She looked up when Aziz approached.

"I held a seat for you." She indicated the chair next to her, picking up her handbag from it. "In case you want to go talk to Tanska."

Aziz shook his head, glancing back. Tanska's tall form and boisterous voice dominated the hubbub behind them. She was currently bent over to yell in the ear of Horace Plancha, the eighty-year-old bandicoot who currently presided over the Association. He had made little secret of his desire to sell his dry cleaning business and retire to Chevali; some people said he had actually approached Vorvarts about selling their block, but

Aziz hadn't seen that proven.

Tanska had clearly given up her attempts to convince a majority of the membership and had chosen to aim at the head, but Horace was as stubborn as Tanska was loud. Even from the front of the room, with the rest of the members trying to talk over the large tiger, Aziz could hear her arguments. "This association is supposed to represent all of us." Horace's reply wasn't audible, but Tanska came back with, "So it's the tyranny of the majority?"

The bandicoot walked away from her and up to the front of the room, calling in his raspy voice, "Let's come to order." Tanska trailed after him, but he ignored her, and she dropped into the seat beside Aziz, tail lashing. He kept his paws clasped together on his lap, preparing something to say should she turn to him, but she hunched over, staring down between her knees.

Horace led them through the summary of the previous week's minutes, during which the silence between his sentences grew more and more tense. Finally he said, "No use beating around the bush. Let's talk about the sale. Here's how we're gonna do this: I'm gonna introduce the topic and then we'll have one speaker for and one against, three minutes each. There'll be ten minutes of open debate and then we're gonna vote." He sighed as Tanska's paw shot up immediately. "Yes? Is this a question of procedure, or..."

"Will the vote have to be unanimous?"

"I'm getting to that," Horace said. "That'll be part of introducing the topic."

He went on to talk about the Vorvarts offers, to stress that nobody needed to reveal the particular amount of their offer, and to say that Vorvarts had told him they would prefer to have unanimous agreement on the sale, but that they could move ahead with their plans even if there were a few holdouts. "They didn't tell me if there were certain key properties they needed, but then, they wouldn't. They did say..." He paused to look down. "That if the entire block sold, they would be able to build a community center for general use."

"Oh, that's great," Tanska said. "Bribing us. What good is a 'community center' if they're gutting the community?" She made air quotes with two fingers.

"A lot, actually," Doug said. "A lot of us host community groups in our stores, and this would give them a place to meet. That's one question I was going to ask."

"All right," Horace said. "Let's try to keep order. One speaker against,

I'm assuming that's you." He gestured to Tanska, who nodded. "And for?"

To Aziz's surprise, Halifa raised her paw. He didn't see who else behind him might have also volunteered, but Horace looked in their direction and indicated her. "All right."

Aziz could feel Tanska's eyes glaring at the back of his head, so he didn't turn. But he couldn't avoid her stare when Horace called her up to the front to deliver her remarks. "I know very few of you agree with me. You think I'm arguing against progress. I know I can't hold back Vorvarts forever. I'm just hoping for another five to ten years. I love this community, and I look across the street at what Vorvarts did to our neighbors, and I don't want that to happen here. I miss my customers Marci and Jose, who like hundreds of others were evicted when their building was sold, and I don't want to lose Doug's bookstore or Angel's tea shop. I don't want to be the only holdout in the shadow of a great big glass monstrosity without any community around me. I don't have cubs, but I know many of you wanted to pass on your shops to your family. How will you do that now?

"But it's about more than that. It's about culture changing. They have their Homeporium already, but they're not happy with that. They have to take over every corner of our world. If we stop them here, maybe we'll get known for it. Maybe we'll be able to hold onto our community, our friends and neighbors, and actually give people an appreciation for what we've had here before it's gone."

As she got wrapped up in her own commentary, her attention drifted from Aziz to glare out at the whole crowd. There was a smattering of applause as she stepped down, in which Aziz joined. Tanska ignored him as she took her seat, staring straight ahead at the podium, not even raising her eyes when Halifa stepped up to it.

Aziz leaned forward, as fascinated by what his wife was going to say as everyone else in the room. She started by surveying the room, met his eyes briefly, and then looked toward the back of the room. "My husband and I came to this neighborhood twenty-three years ago," she said, "and not everyone wished to welcome us in then. There were those who wished to preserve the community as it was. Now we are faced with a different choice. Yes, it is a very drastic choice. It is not the same as welcoming two immigrants to a neighborhood. But the world is changing. We miss the antique stores and coffee shops we've lost, but the new development also has lovely restaurants, a movie theater, and several independent stores. A new development here will allow new people to come in and move the neighborhood into the future. We have all received fair offers for our properties; if progress diverts around us, who can say whether that value will remain? By being afraid to step into the future, we may be dooming ourselves to live forever in the past.

"As for our cubs." She did not look at Aziz. "What we've been offered for our businesses will more than ensure they will have prosperous lives in whatever manner they choose. They need not be tied to our choices."

She stepped down and walked past Aziz's chair on the way to her own. Horace stepped back up and called people for debate, but Aziz didn't listen to them. He leaned over to his wife. "'Need not be tied to our choices,' eh?"

"Aziz." She looked at him reproachfully. "I did not commit us to a decision. I simply spoke my feelings to the group, as I've spoken them to you. What's wrong with that?"

"This isn't about the store," he said. "Have you been talking to him?"

"We are here to vote on whether to sell the store. Nothing more." But the double meaning danced in her eyes.

A response formed in his throat, but he caught it before it escaped. "This is not the place," he said.

"No." She composed herself, looking forward. Behind Aziz, Tanska had stood to yell at someone in the back, and Horace was pleading with her to sit down. Aziz leaned back in his chair, also staring in front of him though his eyes weren't seeing the classroom.

"Oh," Halifa said. "I am having a late dinner with Bea and Lapis. I expect we will discuss President's League business afterwards. I expect I'll be home quite late."

"Fine." To forestall an argument about her speech, no doubt. That was fine. Aziz curled and uncurled his paws and then abruptly got up.

Horace stopped in the middle of whatever he was saying. Tanska registered surprise and then a flicker of hope. Aziz couldn't meet her eyes. "I apologize," he said. "I have been called away. I leave the disposition of our store to my wife. I am sure she will make the correct business decision."

Tanska looked as though he'd punched her in the stomach. Aziz turned, his tail wrapped around his thigh, and strode out of the meeting room.

Chapter Seven: Gerald

Outside, the air had cooled, or else it felt cooler on his fur than the air he was leaving. He stayed to the outside of the sidewalk to avoid the crowds that bustled through the neighborhood. It seemed busy to him until he turned back onto his own street and saw the crowds flowing through the spaces of the Homeporium. Well, soon enough they would have more space to walk. Vorvarts had shared some of their plans for the expansion, which included lovely pedestrian bridges across Nassau St. In practice, Aziz had been told by Tanska, the bridges would never look as good as the plans. They would have budget cuts or overruns and the artistic touches were the first to go.

It was no longer his problem. He would sign the papers sometime this week, as would everyone else, and then they would take their money and scatter. Would he and Halifa stay in the same house? They were bound as husband and wife, but as important as those bonds had been in their homeland and the Upper Devos of twenty-plus years ago, they were both older now, and as Halifa had said, society had changed. Aziz knew three couples in his mosque who had divorced, and though they were not proud of it, neither were they shunned by the community. In all three cases, they'd explained quite reasonably that the marriage no longer benefited either party, and they had mutually agreed to end it (though Halifa told him that at least in one case that was not true).

Perhaps that was where he and Halifa now stood. But again, Aziz did not know what he would do if he didn't go home to his wife every night. The prospect of doing the same routine with a different store, coming home to an empty house, felt hollow to him. He could find charities, he supposed, or some other cause, but the prospect fatigued him. He had worked hard to set up the routine of his life, and it would take a great effort to change it. In the end, he hadn't even been capable of making that decision on his own; he'd left it to Halifa.

Benjamin's emotion, both in person and on the tape, had also jarred him out of his routine. And he'd made a promise during the evening prayer that he had to follow up on, even if he wasn't in much of a mood to talk to Gerald. Although, he thought as he walked, striking up a conversation and guiding it toward marriages and problems would likely be easy for him right now.

After one wrong turn, he got out his phone and looked up Founder's, and three blocks later saw the tea shop and liquor store. From there he had no more trouble. At the door, though, he hesitated. The rainbow flag decal: he knew what that meant. It wasn't a surprise for Gerald to have come in here. But what if someone he knew saw him going in? How could he explain that he'd been fascinated by the love between Gerald and Benjamin that he'd seen on a private tape, that he wanted to understand it and perhaps help restore it?

As he hesitated, the door swung open and a young lion just growing out his mane came out in a burst of conversation and beer smell. "Oh, sorry," he said, holding the door. "Go ahead."

"Thank you," Aziz inclined his head. Because the door was open, he stepped past the lion and into the bar.

For a moment, he expected the conversation to stop, all eyes to turn to him, like in an old Western movie. But nobody took any notice of him. The patrons were exclusively male as far as he could see, paired at high bar tables or sitting in groups of three, four, or five around lower round tables. The wood-paneled walls hung with old black and white pictures, many of which seemed to be of parades or riots or both. Over the bar, a rainbow flag hung suspended from both ends, and rainbow streamers bracketed it on both sides.

Aziz didn't want to just stand in front of the door; eyes *were* beginning to turn to him now. So he walked in, intending to look for Gerald, but he was a foot from the bar before he caught sight of the cougar sitting alone at a table below a window glowing dimly from outside neon. Before he could move toward that wall, the kangaroo behind the bar caught his eye. "What can I get you?"

"Ah…" Aziz shook his head. "Club soda, please."

"Coming up." The bartender grabbed a water glass, scooped it full of ice, and sprayed club soda over top of the ice cubes. He slid it across the wet wooden bar to Aziz. "First time here?"

"Yes. Thank you." Aziz took the glass. "How much?"

The kangaroo waved him off. He spoke with a light Oceanian accent, muted like Aziz's own accent. "On the house. Got an idea what you're looking for? I know most of the regulars here. Save you a bit of time."

The bear to his right perked an ear, curious as well. Aziz glanced his way. "Ah, 'looking for'?"

"Sure." The kangaroo grinned. "Come here alone but don't want to leave alone, right? Don't have a phone out so you're not checking Grindr right away, and if you didn't do that when you walked in then you're not on it. So, you want a bottom or a top? Young or old? Big or little? Bondage? Harder stuff?"

"It's his first time," the bear growled. "And he's drinkin' club soda. He ain't gonna want harder stuff." His accent was pure Upper Devos.

Aziz sipped his soda to give himself time to process this. He had a vague idea what "top" and "bottom" meant, but wasn't anxious to ask or find out by any other means. He was about to excuse himself when an idea occurred to him. "What about that one?" he said. "Cougar in the military gear."

"Ugh." The bear rolled his eyes and went back to his beer.

"Gerald's maybe someone you should save for a month or two down the road," the kangaroo said kindly. "When you've got a couple notches— couple more notches on your belt."

"Why?" Aziz creased his brow.

"One minute." The kangaroo took an order from a grey fox at the other end of the bar.

"Because," the bear growled, "he just comes in here, doesn't talk to nobody, doesn't leave with nobody, just sits with his drink all night long taking up a table."

"What's wrong with that? I'm sorry. I don't know the customs here."

"S'okay." The bear rested his paw on the bar and tapped his claws. "Ray's just tryin' to protect you. Figure if you go over and Ger growls and tells you to get outta his face, you might get the wrong idea about this place. We might growl, but most of us are pretty nice."

"I see." Aziz rubbed his finger along the coolness of his glass. "Perhaps I'll go talk to him, but I promise if he's rude, I won't think badly of the rest of you. All right?"

The bear's shoulder rose and fell. "It's your time. Waste as much as you want."

"The thing about Gerald is," the kangaroo—Ray—said, coming back, "he's married."

"That ain't why he's not hooking up," the bear growled.

"Clyte, you wanna keep your comments to snacks and beer? Something you know something about?"

"You want me to start talking about this shit you call beer?"

"Preaching to the choir," Ray said, indicating the bear's glass. "Where I come from we wouldn't use this shit to mop the floor."

Aziz cleared his throat. "Thanks very much for the help," he said. "I think I will go talk to him, and if he's rude then I'll come back for your advice."

"Good luck." Ray raised a paw and waved with a cheerful smile. "If you can get a half dozen words out of him, you're a better fellow than me or Clyte."

Aziz navigated the tables holding his club soda until he arrived a few feet from Gerald, where he stopped. What was the etiquette? Should he just sit down? Before he could make another move, Gerald rumbled, "I'm not interested."

"What?"

The cougar raised his head and met Aziz's eyes. "Not interested." He enunciated the words clearly. "Go away."

It flashed through Aziz's mind that that was more than a half-dozen words, but that wasn't his goal. "I'm not here to hook up," he said, hoping he was using the phrase properly. "I just want to talk to you."

Gerald groaned and leaned back, his head flopping over the back of the chair. His tail curled and uncurled quickly, whacking the wall. "Did Ben send you? Lion Christ, I told him no more counselors."

"I'm not a counselor either."

The cougar brought his head up and looked at Aziz, really looked at him. His eyes rested on the club soda and then traveled back up to the cheetah's face, getting more interested. "Were you in the service? Over there?"

Aziz shook his head. Gerald fell back, disappointment obvious in the flattening of his ears. "What the hell do you want, then?"

"I told you. I want to talk to you." When Gerald didn't respond, Aziz went on. His back was starting to hurt, so he put all his energy into this last attempt to connect. "You come here often enough that the bartender and customers know you as someone who doesn't want to talk. So why come to this bar full of people?" The cougar continued his bored disinterest. Aziz took a breath. It probably wouldn't be prudent to mention Benjamin, so he was left with only two other possibilities, and he couldn't talk about the persistent image of the shirtless cougar to anyone, especially Gerald himself. "I wonder if it is for the same reason I came here."

Gerald's ear flicked. After a moment, he said, "All right, I'll bite. Why'd you come here?"

"Because I couldn't think of anywhere else to go."

The cougar grunted. After two seconds of thought, his paw gestured toward the chair across from him. Aziz took that for permission and sat down, setting his club soda in front of him and exhaling in relief.

"I thought you were in the service," Gerald said, gesturing to the club soda. "Because you're not drinking. A lot of guys come out of the service and go through AA."

He must have smelled the lack of alcohol. "Not you?" Aziz inclined his head toward Gerald's beer.

The cougar shook his head and took another sip. "Keeps me loose. What's your story?"

"My, ah." The cheetah placed both his paws flat on the table. "My religion forbids it."

Gerald tilted his head, and then his eyes widened as he processed that. "Muslim?" At Aziz's quick nod, he said, "Hell, don't worry. I was over there fighting, but I ain't one of those guys who thinks all of you are terrorists. But…" He squinted. "What're you doing in a gay bar? What branch of Islam are you?"

Aziz took a drink to make sure he wouldn't blurt out anything about Benjamin or the tape. "Sunni Islam. And for why I'm here…someone opened the door," he said, "and I walked in."

"Hah." Gerald smiled for the first time. "But it's not cool with your religion either, is it? It's…" he searched for the word. "*Haraam*? Even with the Sunnis?"

Surprise widened Aziz's eyes. "Yes," he said. "But only to act on one's desires. To have the desires is not something we can prevent. But I, ah…" He was going to tell Gerald that he didn't have the desires, and yet that felt as though he would be distancing himself from Gerald.

"That's not helpful." Gerald broke into his hesitation, then shook his head. "Sorry. I don't feel like debating religion. You do you."

For a moment, Aziz parsed that as a reference to masturbation, but a moment later remembered the colloquialism. "I only recently realized this about myself," he said, playing along because Gerald was sympathetic, figuring out how to turn the conversation to relationships. "But I don't know how to handle it. I can't talk to anyone at my mosque about it, and I can't talk to my wife."

"Wife, huh?" The cougar shook his head. "How long you been married?"

"Twenty-nine years."

Gerald stopped, the beer halfway to his muzzle, and set it down again. "You don't look old enough," he said. "You're just realizing you feel like this now? You never looked at guys before?"

"I did, sure." Aziz coughed and covered his mouth. "But that's not—I mean, there are problems with my marriage."

"So you finally, what, looked at some gay porn? Or did you always do that and just didn't admit you enjoyed it?"

"I never did." Aziz tried to keep the stiffness out of his voice. "Well—for a long time. I did a few years ago, but I thought it was—forgive me—disgusting."

The cougar inclined his head. "I've been there. I thought gay porn was gross until I was fifteen or so and actually tried it."

Aziz's tail curled. He shifted his weight in the chair. "I've known gay people. But recently I met a…" A "married couple" would be skirting too close to the truth, but he'd started the sentence now and his tongue, diverted from its original intent, filled in words seemingly on its own. "A jackal who was my son's lover."

"Whoa." Gerald leaned forward, close enough that Aziz could smell the beer on his breath. "Your son's gay too?"

Now he constructed the lie in his head and his tongue complied. Lying was not something he felt good about doing, but he wrapped it in a veil of telling someone else's true story, and that kept the sense of wrongness at bay. "I wanted to talk to him about his faith and how he could—how he could reconcile. But my wife—my wife is very devout. She insisted we sever all contact with him."

"Hate those religious fanatic types. No offense to your wife, but she sounds like a bitch. Throwing out her own son?"

"Her…her faith is very important to her. As it is to me. Do you have a faith?"

Gerald shook his head slowly. "Used to go to church growing up. Kinda fell away from it." He shrugged lightly. "Don't miss it, to be honest."

"Don't you wish you could talk to someone spiritual?" Aziz gestured with a paw. "I wish I could. None of my spiritual leaders would understand. I can't turn to anyone except people in here."

"And not all the people in here are friendly toward Muslims," Gerald said, looking around as though he could spot the non-friendly people right away. "Lucky you sat down next to me." His brow wrinkled. "Was it luck? Did Ben actually send you?"

"No, I promise. I don't know Ben."

The cougar relaxed. "Well, maybe Allah's looking out for you, then."

Aziz bowed his head out of reflex and murmured, "*Subh*ān Allāh," under his breath. Then he looked up at the cougar. "You've mentioned

Ben twice."

"Yeah." Gerald withdrew, hunching his shoulders.

Again, Aziz held his tongue. Twenty years in a pawnshop had taught him that silence got people to talk more readily than questions, but it was a hard technique for him to use, even with all those years of practice, when he was interested in a conversation. "Yeah," the cougar repeated. "Ben. Well, let me tell you. Me and Ben, we're proof that a good relationship ain't just about finding someone who turns you on."

Flashing back to the tape helped Aziz stay silent while Gerald gathered his thoughts. "We got married quick," he said finally, paws cupped around the beer glass he stared down into. "We'd been dating three months and it was great. 'Fireworks,' Ben would say. He loves romantic books and movies. I like a good action flick, get the blood pumping. Well. Usedta, anyway." He exhaled. "That's another story. So I was going off to the war, and you know, there's always a chance…I mean, we're the best army in the world, and things aren't really hot anywhere, but you never know. Drive over an IED one day and…" He made an explosion noise, his paws flying away from the beer glass and returning to cup it.

"In my home country," Aziz said into the pause, "not where I was, but a few hundred miles to the south, there was always fighting. But not with explosives. Just guns."

"Right." Gerald was deep into his own story. "Y'ever lose anyone to the war?"

"No."

"Lucky. I lost a friend…but that's still another story. Ben. So anyway, Ben wants to get married before I ship out, like in a romantic movie. And I'm…I'm pretty head over tail for him at this point, so I say yes and we do it and it was pretty great. Then I left."

"You had," Aziz clamped his muzzle shut over the rest of the question about their honeymoon and said instead, "to leave right away?"

"Pretty much. That's why we did it, y'know? But it was great, Ben's great. We wrote e-mails back and forth and it made me feel good to have someone waiting for me. Made me maybe a little more careful. I had a couple buddies who fooled around with some girls there, but…"

Into the pause, Aziz said, "Another story?"

"Hah. And how. But anyway, I got back a year and a half ago. We had some trouble with money right away. Ben lost his job and my paperwork with the VA kept getting stuck. And Ben just kept talking about how it was fine because we had each other. I was having trouble adjusting and I couldn't get my therapy set up because of the goddamned VA, and I kept focusing on practical things like where we were going to get food from."

"That seems reasonable."

"Thanks," the cougar said. "I thought so. But Ben didn't want to take a job just to put money on the table. He's trained as a social worker, and he's been looking for more jobs in that area. The problem is there are so many people out here who want to do that job that there's a long process. He'd rather work for a non-profit and make no money than take some kind of custodial job that would at least make it easier to pay our rent."

"So you have to make all the money?" Aziz asked.

"Not anymore. I finally convinced him to take a bartending class and now he's got a good job at Clancy's over on Bellmont. I got a small pension from the army and I'm working down at the shooting range on Firefly. You know it?"

Aziz shook his head. "I stay mostly to Upper Devos."

"What do you do?" Gerald inclined his head.

"I own a store." The words came out before he could stop them. Only then did he realize that Ben might have told Gerald about the cheetah who'd gotten their camera back. What could he say he owned instead of a pawnshop? An antique store?

But Gerald didn't ask, just nodded his head. "I don't get over to Upper Devos much. There's a coffee shop there that one of my old army buddies turned me on to, but other than that I stick to Cottage Hill."

"So you've both got jobs," Aziz said before the cougar could ask him more about his store. "So things are getting better?"

Slowly Gerald shook his head. "When we were having money troubles, I thought maybe our problems were about that. But now the money's coming in, and because his job has weird hours, we don't have a lot of time together. What we do have he wants to spend indoors watching movies cuddled up on the couch. I like going out and seeing things. I get restless if I'm indoors too long. I don't know if that's a change because I was in the war or what. I think I was like that before, but I cared about him so much I could talk myself into doing whatever he wanted and I'd be happy just to spend time with him. Now…"

Aziz picked up his club soda and sipped. Gerald let out a sigh. "Nothing as dramatic as like what you were talking about. But I don't feel that magic anymore. I think Ben does, but it makes me feel guilty and sad when he tries to do romantic things and I'm not feeling it."

Like bringing a honeymoon tape back. Aziz wondered if Ben had tried showing Gerald the tape yet. "A marriage is more than romance," he said. "A marriage is an agreement between a husband and—between two people. You don't just abandon it if there is trouble."

"Yeah, yeah, Ben's read me that speech already." Gerald narrowed his eyes. "What if there's nothing there anymore in a marriage? What if there might be someone else out there who understands you better, someone else who's right for you? And it's not anyone's fault, it's just that you've changed, and he's changed, or maybe you've changed and he hasn't and that's the problem. How long do you have to try to work it out before you give up?"

Nothing came to Aziz's tongue. "I don't know," he said after a moment.

"Yeah, you got the same problem, only you got a religious angle to it. I can't help you with that. Parents didn't take me to church much, and when I figured out I was gay, well…" He laughed.

"If you don't mind me asking," Aziz said, "how did you figure it out?"

"No big trick." The cougar finished his beer. "Like I said, I thought gay porn was gross, but I wasn't interested in straight porn at all. Then a friend of mine came out as gay in my high school class. He said he thought I was hot but he understood if I didn't feel the same. And I couldn't stop thinking about him. So we started hanging out. Hooked up once or twice, and then, I dunno, I started meeting more people."

"And this was…" Gerald frowned at him, and Aziz clarified. "How old were you?"

"Oh. Sixteen. Well, fifteen when I started looking on the Internet for gay porn. To be disgusted at." He cleared his throat. "It was a really confusing time."

"I can imagine." Aziz folded his paws together. "When I was sixteen, I…" This time he managed to catch himself. That was not a memory to dwell on now. "I was working at my father's market stall. My wife and I were married when I was seventeen and she was thirteen. We had one child and he was three when we came to this country."

"Wow. So you've been here a long time."

"Over twenty years."

"How much has changed?"

His first thoughts turned to the neighborhood they were sitting in, one he only knew a few things about. "We looked at Cottage Hill when we first moved here," he said, "but it was a poorer neighborhood then. The environmental activists had gotten the factory up in Chellah Heights closed, and a lot of the people were out of work. Even then it was a—a gay neighborhood, but I didn't realize it. It wasn't as…" He searched for the word.

"Obvious?"

Aziz nodded. "The people were not so open. There were rainbow flags, but I didn't know what those meant until much later."

"It, ah," Gerald exhaled. "It makes it a lot easier to find people. You know, to have a normal life. I told you about high school, how hard it was to realize who I was. If my friend hadn't come up to me, I might never have met another gay guy for years. Now…" He gestured around to the bar. "I can sit with a whole bunch of them."

"And not talk to any of them?"

The cougar's ears folded down, but he smiled. "Yeah, well. Most of them just want to hit on me or…well, that's about it, really. Not many here who want to have a good conversation."

Aziz felt warm at having produced the smile, and then the moment dragged on. What was happening? He didn't want to break the connection, but didn't want to encourage it either. He reached back for more history, what little he knew. "You know this was a wolf neighborhood, historically."

"Right." Gerald's smile didn't waver. "There's still street names like 'Pack Ave.' and there's like three 'Howl' streets."

"Upper Devos used to be foxes." Aziz relaxed. Just innocent conversation, that was all it was. "Longer ago. The street names have changed more. Cottage Hill was still heavily canid when we moved here, though not as much as in the sixties. Upper Devos was more diverse at the time. Now I think it's reversed perhaps. In the early 2000s a lot of money came into Cottage Hill and it became a shopping destination. We looked at putting a store in there but couldn't afford it."

"Oh. What kind of store do you own? Sorry if you mentioned it already."

Aziz said, "Pawnshop," before he could stop himself. He went on quickly, trying to blow past the slip. "Cottage Hill was becoming a boutique kind of place. They actually put laws in there preventing anyone from owning a single plot of commercial zoned space over a threshold to keep out the big retail chains that weren't already there. Upper Devos was trying to put in an ordinance like that four years ago, but it didn't pass."

"To stop that big development?"

"The Homeporium, yes."

Gerald shook his head. "That thing is gross."

"It is the way the world is moving. Fifteen years ago everyone wanted to be Cottage Hill: small, independent stores with loyal clientele. People came from all over Port City to visit. Now I could put a store in Cottage Hill if I wanted to, but it doesn't make sense. The rents are far higher than the stores are taking in." Halifa had done much of that research months before, when they'd looked at their options in the wake of the Vorvarts offer.

"I don't think there are many pawnshops in Cottage Hill. You might do okay."

Aziz hurried to get off the subject of pawnshops. "I don't know when I realized Cottage Hill was a gay neighborhood. Or at least, had a large gay population. I think it was just a few years ago. Like I said, it was not always so obvious, and in the past decade I have mostly kept to Upper Devos." That wasn't true of Marquize, but…that was another matter, and it wasn't Gerald's business. "Did you grow up here?"

"Oh, no." Gerald's ears flicked back and then forward. "I grew up in western Upland, coal country. Ben's from here, so I moved here when I got back. Wasn't much for me in Upland anymore anyway."

"How did you meet?" Here, at last, he might be getting to their marriage and their problems.

"That's a long story. Might need another beer for it. You want anything? It's on me." Gerald got up, and Aziz shook his head. He stared down at his glass, wondering how long he was going to sit here talking, why he felt more able to open up to Gerald than to most of his other friends.

"Hey." The cougar had only stood up, hadn't moved beyond the table. He looked upset, his ears flat, tail lashing.

The cheetah set his own ears back instinctively, very aware now of how much more muscular Gerald was than him. "What's wrong?"

"Pawnshop." Gerald's eyes stared down. "Did I…did I bring the camera into your shop?"

He wanted badly to lie, to smooth things over. He couldn't force the lie past his throat, though. The lie about being more tolerant of Marquize had been hard enough, and that was based in truth, albeit Halifa's truth. To lie now would be worse, and in a sense, facing Gerald's wrath now would be punishment for that lie as well. "Yes," he admitted.

Gerald's lips were tight, his muzzle bunched in a near-snarl. "That means you must have been the one Ben went to to get it back."

Aziz's tongue felt twice its normal size. He gulped and couldn't get any words out. Gerald's paw landed on his shoulder with a hard, unforgiving grip. "So what's your game? Did you find out we were having trouble? Figured you'd swoop in on me here, get me off guard with a little conversation?"

"N-no. I didn't want—"

"Why didn't you tell me first thing? Oh. Because you don't come over here. You wouldn't have known me unless…you watched the tape, is that it?" He gave Aziz only a second, not enough for the cheetah to compose any kind of response. An hour might not have been enough time to compose a reasonable response. "Did you watch the whole thing? Had yourself a nice little jerk-off to our honeymoon?"

His voice carried, or else the bar had fallen silent, or perhaps both. "Please," Aziz said. "It's not—"

"But that wasn't enough. So you figured you'd come find me. Did you follow me here? Or have you been asking around to see where I go?"

"I saw you on the street," Aziz gasped. "I only wanted—"

Gerald let him go with a shove that almost sent his chair toppling over. "You're not getting it, whatever it is. Just forget it. Fuck off."

The cougar stalked away without looking back. Aziz sat gripping the edges of his chair, willing his heart to slow. The entire bar's eyes moved from him to Gerald as the cougar shoved open the door. When it swung shut again, Aziz felt their attention, though most were courteous enough to keep their eyes and ears from focusing directly on him.

Then a shape loomed over him. He snapped his head up and saw Ray, the kangaroo's brow lowered, eyes dark. "Think you better leave as well," he said. "You're upsetting the customers."

"It was only him." But Aziz was already getting up as he said it, and Ray didn't respond nor follow him as he headed for the door.

Chapter Eight: Coronado

Mortified, he hurried along the streets back to his house, sure that everyone could see his shame, as though the angel on his left were hurrying alongside him scribbling down a record of that conversation. Only when he'd closed the front door after him and leaned back against it, panting, did his chest unclench and his breath come in long, ragged gasps.

Upstairs, he headed for his room, but stopped with a paw on the door. His wife's room was still lit, her door half open. He walked there and peered around the corner at her empty bed. What would he have said to her if she were home? She'd done what he knew had to be done when he himself didn't have the stomach for it. He crept quietly to his room, lost himself in the *isha*, and fell into a fitful sleep.

He woke early, uneasy. After his morning prayer, he spoke a short *du'a* asking for forgiveness for his treatment of Gerald and for his angry thoughts toward his wife. He would ask again in the evening, with his fellows around him to remind him that his community was supportive. The thought crossed his mind that he should seek Gerald out and apologize to him in person, but that could hardly go well, could it?

The sun shone on his walk to the store, and the shame of the previous night almost felt consigned to his past. He'd been an idiot to pursue Gerald anyway. Anything might have happened to him—what if Gerald had been violent and Aziz ended up in the hospital? Not that Halifa couldn't manage the sale on her own, but his signature would also have been needed, and it would have complicated everything.

Perhaps he'd wanted to complicate things. Perhaps he felt uncertain about selling, about abandoning this life to move into the unknown. The worry slowed his steps in front of Tanska's shop, moderately crowded. He had time to stop for a pastry, so he went inside.

The Siberian tiger had a bright smile on for all her customers, dishing out cinnamon-walnut rogaliki and crisp hvorost dusted with powdered sugar alongside donuts and gingerbread, with cups of coffee steaming alongside them. The smells, as always, brought Aziz to lick his lips.

When he made his way to the front of the line, Tanska's smile vanished. "Good morning, sir," she said. "What can I get you?"

"Gingerbread, please. But Tanska, I wanted to talk about—"

In the time it took him to say half a sentence, she snatched a piece of gingerbread with her tongs, slid it into a brown paper bag, and pushed it across the counter. "Three dollars, please."

"And a coffee."

She turned away from him to fill a cup from the urn behind the counter. "Tanska," he tried again, "we should talk about what's going to happen…"

When she brought the coffee alongside the gingerbread, her muzzle remained expressionless. "Four fifty total."

He laid a five on the counter. "Please talk to me."

She held out two quarters; he took them and dropped them in the tip jar. "Yes, ma'am?" Tanska said to the female leopard behind him.

"Tanska—"

"I'm very busy, sir," she said, and then returned her attention to the leopard.

So Aziz took his gingerbread and coffee down the street to his shop and breathed in the strong coffee smell as he prepared to open. He made his usual circuit of the shelves to ensure that nothing looked out of place, touched some of the items he particularly remembered and thought about the people who'd owned them. Cameras, musical instruments, pieces of art (fine and pop culture), jewelry, computer equipment, handbags, place settings and dishes, pieces and fragments of a thousand other lives. Gerald and Tanska were only two people in the great big world, he reminded himself as he returned to his computer and register and made sure that both were ready.

But when a red fox pushed the door open a little after nine-thirty, Aziz tensed until he saw that it wasn't Benjamin. He usually read the news on his computer while the store wasn't busy, but today his eyes kept flicking up from the screen to the crowd outside, Whenever a cougar passed, Aziz felt a mixture of excitement and dread, his heart sped up, and his paws tensed. But none of the cougars was Gerald, and none of the foxes was Benjamin, and by the time seven-thirty came around, he closed early and walked to the coffee shop.

It wasn't until he was on the patio looking for a table that he remembered that Gerald also came to that café. But the cougar was nowhere to be seen, and Doug was waving him over with a large reddish paw.

Aziz slumped into the chair across from the squirrel. "You're early," Doug said. "Slow day?"

The squirrel looked as though he'd already retired, sitting across from Aziz with an easy smile, his shirt hanging open to show off his bright red chest fur, and a casual swish to his tail. Aziz's own tail felt as tightly coiled as a spring. "Rather slow. But this Vorvarts thing is on my mind."

Doug cocked his head. "Because of Tanska?" Aziz nodded. "She's going to have to make her own way. You can't solve her problems for her."

"But why not? Isn't that what community does?"

The squirrel sighed. "Yes. When we can. But sometimes someone is determined to go contrary to the community, and then you can't waste too much time trying to get them back. Look: she feels like we're rejecting her, so she's rejecting us to get back the upper paw. She doesn't want to come back to the community now; she wants to feel like she's left it on her own terms."

"I don't know," Aziz said. "She's very upset. I think she would be happiest if the whole Vorvarts deal went away."

"She hasn't made a secret of that. I'd be happiest if my prostate worked properly. We can't always get what we want."

Aziz sighed and smiled. "Perhaps you're right. But she's our friend. Will she stay with her pastry shop on this corner as they build around her?"

"They're not going to build around her. They're going to go after her."

Aziz's eyebrows rose. He felt a chill as though a cloud had passed over the sun. "Are you serious? Horace said they had plans, that they didn't need…"

Doug's smile had no humor in it. "They're not going to give up the block for one holdout. They've got a team of lawyers that probably makes more than what they've offered us for our shops. They'll get her pastry shop. Probably the days of people planting mice in restaurants are over, but the legal tricks they have are just as dirty."

"I know from…" Aziz gestured toward the Homeporium. "But they said this time it would be different."

"It's never different. It's always about the bottom line. But why worry? You and Halifa are going to sell and I am too. Which reminds me…"

Aziz sipped his tea, ears perked. Doug took out his phone and set it on the table. Aziz leaned over to see pictures of a bright blue sky, a beach with golden sand and turquoise water, slender people of all species in skimpy beachwear, white stucco houses with red clay roofs in an Old World style. "This is Coronado, some pictures my son sent me. It's nice there, sunny most of the time, near the beach, no harsh winters like here.

I decided I'm going to take him up on his offer." He grinned. "I've always wanted to watch the sun set over the ocean."

"You're moving to Coronado?"

The squirrel nodded. "I put my place up on the market today."

"Wow." Aziz looked around the café again. "So no more café."

"The shop will still be here. You can call me on the phone. Just remember it's three hours earlier out there." The squirrel winked. "Not that I'll be keeping regular hours or anything."

"How expensive are houses out there?"

Doug raised his eyebrows. Aziz looked past him to the clientele of the café, and his eyes were drawn to the dingo and fox, sitting together again and both looking at their phones. "You and Halifa might want to come out to Coronado?"

"Well." Aziz avoided his friend's eyes. "Halifa has her charity work here. We might buy a house for vacations. Perhaps I would stay there longer."

"Oh." The squirrel brought his coffee cup to his lips and sipped slowly. "I'd enjoy your company, of course."

Aziz often envied Doug's ability to keep from blurting out things. Doug had known for years that he and Halifa had been living separate lives, but Aziz had always stressed that they remained happy, that a marriage allowed both spouses freedom. This was Doug's first hint that they might spend time apart. Honestly, it was the first time Aziz had vocalized it to anyone, but the thought had occurred naturally to him. Of course he and Halifa would miss each other, but they barely saw each other anymore anyway. And with the events of the past day, Aziz would as soon make a clean break.

He looked again at the dingo and fox, now both watching something on the fox's phone with broad smiles. "We haven't discussed anything, but…she's been talking about moving on to new things." Doug nodded, but didn't say anything. "We live separate lives," Aziz said. "And I think she's been talking to Marquize."

"Oh?" Doug lifted his head. "Why do you think that?"

"Because of what she said at the meeting." Aziz shifted in his chair. "Of course she can talk to him if she wants, but I asked her not to. He turned his back on us and on Islam and if we act as though that means nothing, it demeans our faith and our family."

"I know."

"Sorry." Aziz pushed his tea away and clasped his paws together, fingers intertwined. His tail curled around a chair leg tightly. Around him, the café remained completely unconcerned by his dilemma. "The sale is bringing all this back, and the camera I told you about."

"Right, the husband with the camera." Doug leaned forward. "Something happened with that?"

"Yes. I mean." Aziz shook his head. "I ran into his husband. We talked. He seems like a nice fellow."

The squirrel raised an eyebrow. "Where did you run into him?"

"Here, actually." Aziz gestured to the patio. "Benjamin—the fox—described his husband as a cougar with a military background, and I saw a cougar in army clothes here, so I spoke with him."

"Uh-huh. And did you tell him why you were speaking with him?"

"No." Aziz scowled at Doug's smile. "I was curious. Someone comes into your store with a story, you want to know the rest of it."

"I see. And did you find out?"

"Some of it, yes." The cheetah glanced around, but still Gerald was nowhere in evidence. "They're having problems. I didn't pry."

"Mm."

Doug's silence prompted Aziz to keep talking. "Their problems are like any married couple."

"Sure. Gay couples aren't any different." Doug gestured at him. "You and Halifa aren't exactly a traditional married couple where one spouse works and the other doesn't."

Aziz didn't say anything, thinking about all the ways in which he'd thought his family was traditional, until Halifa started spending more time away from the shops, until Marquize betrayed them. "We may be traditional in the manner of a TV or movie drama," he said. "The dysfunctional States family."

When Doug didn't say anything, Aziz remembered why he didn't discuss his family very often. "I'm sorry," he said.

"It's fine." Doug waved a paw. "It's been years. I'm at peace. But that's partly why it'll be nice to be nearer Thom. And he says there's a small Prevost's community out there. More than here, anyway. He's seeing someone."

"Oh, that's good to hear. Maybe you'll be there for a grandkit."

"That's my hope. But I'm happy just to relax by the beach. I want to be one of those old guys who sits on the beach all day drinking coffee and watching all the young cute females go by. You know there's a nude beach there, Thom says?"

"No!" Aziz laughed. "I've heard of those things but I can't imagine it myself."

"Come out to Coronado, you won't have to."

"But…wouldn't we have to be nude as well?"

The squirrel beamed at him with a gleam in his eye. "At our age, you don't think that a fair trade?"

"I suppose you may be right. I'll talk to Halifa." Aziz's smile faltered.

Doug nodded slowly. "I don't know if it's any consolation, Zeez. But you know, there's life after marriage."

"It's different," Aziz said. "Not more painful, but harder to know why it happened. Was it always fated to end? Was it because of Marquize, and if so, was it because of how she handled or or how I handled it? Or was it because—"

The fox and dingo were holding paws now, talking low with smiles on their muzzles. Aziz broke off and stared at them, then jerked his gaze back to Doug.

"You can't know why it happened." Doug's voice was quiet, his muzzle creased in sympathy. "But you also can't wonder how many more years you might have had. You're at a fork in the road and you're choosing to take a branch. Are things really at that point?"

"Maybe not. We've had fights before. But we had a spark back then, or at least…" A son to keep them together. "Something."

"The sale is a good chance to take stock of your life, re-evaluate." A small smile curved the squirrel's lips. "Start a new adventure, perhaps."

"It's not as easy as in a book. The heroes in your adventures, they don't have property to dispose of, houses to sell, businesses to manage." Aziz's tail had unwound from the chair leg now, though, and he relaxed against the back of the chair. "But thank you for talking to me about it. It's much harder when it's all in here." He tapped his head, feeling slightly guilty because there was still the one issue that was trapped in his head where he didn't dare talk to anyone about it.

"I know how that is." Doug nodded. "You know, when Palia died, I went to a support group. They probably have one for troubled marriages. I can get you the number if you want."

Aziz shook his head and then thought better of it. "That would be helpful, I think. Thank you."

Chapter Nine: Apologies

He got the number from Doug and then excused himself to attend his evening prayers. But all the way to the mosque he wondered whether there had been a message to him in Doug's decision to move to Coronado, to leave his life here behind and try something new. Or maybe the message had been in the dingo and fox in his line of sight as Doug had been talking. This was different from the uneasiness he'd felt in the presence of gay couples in the past; in the past he hadn't thought as fixedly about any of them as he was now thinking about Gerald, dreading and hoping that the cougar would appear around the next corner.

The presence of the others in the mosque soothed him. He greeted them, clasped paws, and breathed in the scented water they all used to wash. Here, if nowhere else, was a community where even if he had little in common with the other members, he could always come and pray with them, be surrounded by their communal faith, and remember that the world turned under the same eye. Again, following his prayers, he spoke in his head a *du'a*, not for forgiveness this time, but for understanding. Why was the cougar so foremost in his mind, and was that why he was already envisioning the end of his marriage? Or was Halifa's behavior and their increased estrangement finally sinking in?

He concluded his prayer, one of the last to do so, and rose. Around him, everyone else had formed small groups, talking animatedly as they often did. And as was his recent custom, Aziz moved through the groups without talking to any of them. He wondered whether there was a mosque in Coronado. There had to be at least a small community that prayed together. He could look that up online, he supposed, or on his phone if he cared, but he didn't need to know right this minute.

On the way out, he paused to look at the community bulletin board. There was a meeting the following night to plan activities to promote the mosque in the area. The fennec who'd arranged those activities when Aziz and Halifa had first come here had stepped aside long before, and had passed away some seven years ago. His successor, a nice enough oryx, had recently passed the torch along to a younger, more energetic oryx, whose horns could often be seen waving above the crowds during meetings. Ashtari, Aziz thought his name was, had approached both him and Halifa a few years ago at the worst possible time and had seemed personally offended at their polite refusal to help. Aziz had also said, probably a result both of his quick tongue and his foul mood at the time, that he had been watching community events here for two decades and that nothing substantial had come of them.

At least it had proven effective in stopping Ashtari from bothering them after that. He gave the flyer one last look, somewhat envious of the energy and vision of these younger Muslims, and then stepped outside.

A light drizzle had come up, fogging the sky and blurring the lines of the people around him. Aziz flattened his ears and hurried along the street, following the crowd. His mind stayed back at the mosque though, with the prayer he'd made. This was another test, another trial, coming along with the imminent sale, and he had to endure it. Gerald wouldn't be around forever, and after a few days these strange feelings should be as gone as the cougar was. If he couldn't sort out the tangle in his head, he'd run off to Coronado, would work it out with Halifa somehow. She could talk to Marquize all she wanted with him out of the picture.

He wiped rain from his eyes and checked the street sign. He was at Larchmont and Swartern, and normally he would keep going another two blocks and be almost home. But Larchmont was familiar for some reason; he'd seen the name recently. He stood, moisture collecting on his ears and the top of his head, and finally decided that perhaps this was the sign he'd been waiting for. So he turned left down Larchmont, keeping his eyes up now, looking for something, anything that might be significant to him.

This area he knew a little better than the Cottage Hill neighborhood; it was still Upper Devos, albeit getting close to the Cottage Hill boundary. He didn't want to chance heading back towards Founders, but this was a different area, so even if he did cross over, he didn't risk running into anyone who'd seen him at that bar.

How far would he go, though? He paused in the awning of a closed locksmith's shop and stared across the street at the river of people flowing by, some with umbrellas out, some simply hurrying through the rain. Though stores dotted the side of the street he was on, the opposite side consisted of several large apartment buildings. Aziz let his gaze wander over the myriad of windows, reflecting that probably the inhabitants of the neighborhood before those buildings had gone up had hated them as much as the current inhabitants hated the Homeporium.

And then as his eyes passed over the windows with their posters, their stickers, the blue lights of television glowing from over half of them, he saw the silhouette of a fox's head on the second floor, and memory rushed back to him. Larchmont: that was the street on Benjamin's driver's license. There were a number of foxes in Upper Devos, of course, and no guarantee that this was Benjamin himself, but Aziz felt as though it had to be. He leaned back against the glass of the window and brought his phone out, pretending to be looking at it as his eyes stayed fixed on the fox in the window.

Benjamin, if it was indeed him, watched TV for about five minutes and then got up and came to the window. Aziz shrank back as the fox looked out into the street, and his posture and movements made Aziz as certain as he could be that this was indeed Benjamin. The fox scanned the street below and waited there for another minute or two before turning, ears down, and slumping back into his chair.

Aziz wanted to ring the doorbell and tell the fox to stop hoping for Gerald to come back, to move on and find someone else. But when he thought about it, what right did he have to dispense that advice, he who moved through this world withdrawn, from house to shop to café to mosque and back to house again, running a circle without stopping? When people dropped away from him he left them behind; Doug and Tanska had been the remaining constants in his life, they and Halifa, who had become like the rain, an ever-present background that he walked through and barely interacted with.

And now Tanska wanted nothing more to do with him, and Doug was moving to Coronado. Aziz could follow him out there, of course. There was a certain appeal to the idea, especially standing in the rain and thinking about the icy cold and slushy streets of the not-too-far-past winter. Warm sand, bright sun, no pressure…no decisions to make, just tea to drink and Doug to talk to.

Did they have all the things he'd grown to love here? Possibly not. But he could grow to love new things.

Across the street, another familiar form rounded the corner. Aziz's breath caught as he recognized Gerald. The cougar's round earswere flat against the rain like his had been, his olive t-shirt wet and sticking to his fur, paws shoved into the pockets of his camo pants. He stopped at the door of the apartment building, stared at it, and then slowly walked on.

Impulsively, Aziz ran across the street to intercept him. Here was his sign, here was his chance. By the time he'd dodged the cars and come up behind Gerald, he had at least the beginnings of what he was going to say in his head, and trusted himself to come up with the rest as he always did.

The cougar, alerted by his footsteps, turned before Aziz could touch him. His ears came up and then flattened again, his muzzle wrinkling as he recognized the cheetah. Aziz put a paw up. "Before you say anything," he said, "I want to apologize. It wasn't right of me to mislead you."

"Have you been following me again?" Gerald didn't look any less angry.

"No. I had your address from when your husband got the camera. I came by and waited so I would have the chance to apologize. That's all." He tried not to look at how tightly the shirt clung to Gerald's chest. "And I did not watch all the tape, only enough to make sure it was the right camera."

Finally, the cougar's expression relaxed. "Well, I appreciate the apology," he said. "Good night."

But his eyes held Aziz's for a moment, those round greenish-brown eyes gleaming with the reflection of the night around them, and Aziz swallowed once before he said, "Good night." He turned and walked quickly through the rain back to his house.

Chapter Ten: Bridges

At home, Halifa had prepared their response to the Vorvarts offer. She and Aziz had a cordial conversation about it, and he agreed that he would take it to the store, sign it, and courier it over the next day. She didn't ask how he felt about the sale, and he thanked her for taking care of the paperwork; nothing more. He retired to his room and thought again about a cougar and a fox holding each other closely as the waves broke and splashed behind them.

The next morning, Aziz took out the letter and spread it carefully on the counter. Halifa had left a space for him to sign next to her. "Co-Owner," it said below both their names. He picked up a pen to sign it three times and put it down each time. And then the store got busy with the mid-morning rush, the people who were out of work coming in to sell off a few of their possessions along with the retirees looking to see what was new, what other people were getting rid of. This morning, Aziz had one of those rare moments when someone browsing happened to want what someone was selling; in this case it was an old goat, Vicunza, who had his eye on an old game console that a young llama had brought. "My son collects those," he told her, and then turned to Aziz. "What were you giving for it?"

"Twenty-five," Aziz said.

Vicunza had been a customer for a long time. "And marked up to fifty, no doubt? Here." He put twenty on the counter, and then offered twenty-five to the llama.

She looked at Aziz. "Is that…"

"It's fine, it's fine." Vicunza kept the money out. "I give Aziz lots of business, I save him a little paperwork. We understand each other."

"It's fine," Aziz assured the llama.

"Oh. All right, then." She set the console down on the counter.

"Here." Vicunza added another five to his stack. "You look like you need it."

She reached out and took the money, holding it for a moment and looking at Aziz as though asking his permission again. He nodded with a smile, and she put the cash into her handbag. "Thank you, both of you," she said again.

"I hope your circumstances improve," Aziz said.

When she'd walked out of the store, Vicunza waved a hand at Aziz. "You got a rag? This thing is all dusty."

Aziz reached below the counter and came out with a cloth. The goat set about wiping down the console, taking care to get into all the cracks. "Phew. At least I don't think she took it away from a kid. What do you think? Husband?"

"Maybe." Aziz's attention was caught by a muscular cougar coming into the shop.

"Looks like he didn't play it much anymore. Or maybe he's out of work and she's getting him to stop. Heh heh. Well…" Vicunza hefted the console. "If he's not going to use it, I know someone who will. Hey, Aziz. You going to sell to those Homeporium people?"

The cougar had stopped just inside the doorway, pretending to look at the rack of DVDs while clearly glancing toward the counter. "I think so," Aziz said to Vicunza. "They made a generous offer. Everyone else is selling—almost."

"Enh." The goat tucked the console under his arm. "Won't be the same without you. But get your money while you can. If they couldn't build here, they'd move to another block and this block would start losing people. Once those people move in, all their people move in with them and the only ones who like the old neighborhood are us old people." He breathed a wheezy laugh. "What are you going to do with the money?"

Aziz shook his head. Gerald—it was him, in a black t-shirt with the "POW*MIA" design on it and those same camo pants—had moved to look at sewing machines. "We don't know yet. A friend offered me a place out in Coronado. Halifa has her charities here. And we have three other stores to think of."

"True, true. Maybe I'll have to take the train out to Cape Red to get my junk fix." Vicunza shifted the console to the other arm. "All right, I'm going to get this home. Thanks, Aziz. Have a good day. Let me know when you're closing, I'll come in and sniff through the discounts."

"Of course." Aziz bowed and smiled.

As the goat pushed the door open, Gerald lifted his head and made his way to the back of the store, slowly, as though he didn't really have anything urgent in mind. His tail was lashing, though, and when he got to the counter, he put his paws on it and looked Aziz right in the eye. "Hey," he said.

"Good morning." Aziz fought to keep his tone polite. He wasn't sure whether he was afraid or excited at what Gerald was going to do. "How may I help you?"

His formality made the cougar pause in whatever speech he had prepared. "It's Gerald? From Founders, and last night?"

"Yes, I recognized you."

"Oh." The cougar's lips twitched in what was almost a smile. "Usually when you recognize someone, you say their name."

"I was not sure you'd appreciate the familiarity."

"Ah. Yeah." Gerald looked down. "I deserve that, I guess. But you still shouldn't have—" He looked around the store. "I mean, you shouldn't have come after me."

"I apologized already." Aziz kept his voice low. "But I will be happy to apologize again. My conduct was not what I would expect of myself."

"No, no." Gerald put a paw up. "I thought about it. I mean, technically you didn't do anything wrong. I sold the camera with the tape in it. Anyone who bought it has the right to look at the tape, even if you had looked at the whole thing." He glanced at Aziz, and the cheetah had the feeling that Gerald thought he really had watched the whole tape. He found himself half-wishing that he had. "I probably should've erased it."

"You knew it was in the camera?" Aziz's eyebrows rose.

Gerald looked away, shuffled his feet, and sighed. "Not…maybe not consciously. But Ben had been looking at the video the previous week, and I…he never took the tapes out when he was done with them. So I told myself that if he'd put it away, he'd still have it, and if he hadn't, it would serve him right." He rubbed behind one ear. "Pretty shitty of me, I know. I don't know why he still wants to be with me."

"A marriage is about more than just one incident, though," Aziz said.

"Yeah, but doesn't that incident…sometimes that signals the way the marriage is going already, doesn't it?"

Aziz considered that, and then Gerald noticed a field mouse holding a stack of CDs waiting her turn. He stepped aside so Aziz could ring up the sale, and then stepped back when the mouse left. "Anyway, I was thinking…if you were watching that tape and thinking about your feelings…well, I know Islam isn't really keen on the whole gay thing. So it must be really difficult, and you probably don't have a lot of people to talk to."

"I don't really need to talk…" Aziz focused on curling his tail in and out, aware that his heart was beating faster. Gerald being close, being concerned about him. "I mean, I'm not…I'm married."

'Yeah. So am I." Gerald held up his paws. "I'm not coming on to you or anything. Just offering an ear to talk."

"That's what…" Aziz closed his eyes, pressed his fingers to them. His ears felt flushed and he felt that he had to choose his words very carefully. "I felt badly about your marriage. I thought I might talk to you about it."

"To me?" Gerald smiled. "Sure, okay, but…" Another customer, a red fox in a blue t-shirt, had stepped up behind Gerald with a brown paper grocery bag full of items to sell. "Look, if you want to meet and talk later, I don't have anything going on tonight."

"Sure," Aziz said without thinking, and then thought, *what am I doing?* "Where?"

"There's a neat little food court in the Homeporium with a patio. How about there?"

"I thought you hated the Homeporium."

"Yeah, well." Gerald glanced back as though the building across the street could hear them talking about it and he didn't want to offend it. "The food court isn't bad, and after hours most of the annoying people are gone."

"All right." His mind spun, but he'd already agreed. "I close the store at eight, have my prayers…I could be there by nine."

"I think they close at nine-thirty or ten. That should be fine. See you then." Gerald raised a paw with a smile, and walked out.

It took a moment for Aziz's heart to slow. What was happening to him? He watched Gerald leave, and only when the door had shut behind the cougar's tail did he turn his attention to the red fox, who was still holding his brown bag. "You want to sell?" Aziz said. "You can put them on the counter."

"Salaam," the fox said, and did so slowly, and then Aziz recognized him: one of the foxes from the Devos Musjid Al-Islam, one of the young ones who'd just joined recently. His heart jumped a gear again.

"Ah, let us see what you have." He let his paws pick through the books, DVDs, and collectibles mechanically as his brain tried to engage. Had the fox heard his conversation? Had he been paying attention? How could Aziz ask that without letting on that there had been something to overhear? And was there anything to overhear? He had only made an appointment to meet a friend for a drink. Gerald had said that he wasn't coming on to Aziz…

And if the fox had heard *that*, what would he think?

He accepted Aziz's evaluation of his things without question, which was another bad sign: people from Devos Musjid Al-Islam, when they came to give Aziz their business, often haggled over a few dollars, not necessarily because they wanted to save the money, but because that was how things were done. Like prayer, it was a custom that eased their interaction, made them feel closer. But when Aziz offered the fox thirty dollars, prepared to go to forty if necessary, the fox simply nodded his head and accepted the cash.

When he was gone, Aziz turned back to the sale document. He signed his name decisively, then sealed it in an envelope and called the courier.

Chapter Eleven: Severance

That evening, Aziz met Doug at the café as usual. After greeting his friend, Aziz tried to keep up his end of the conversation while staring around the café looking for Gerald, until Doug snapped his fingers and drew Aziz's attention. "You don't have to decide about Coronado right away," he said.

"What?"

"Come out and visit. Talk things over with Halifa. Don't sit and brood about it."

"Ah." Aziz seized on the excuse. "I will. It's a large change, you know."

"For me too." Doug smiled. "That's why I'd like to have you along. It would be nice to have one familiar muzzle out there."

"I understand the feeling." Aziz sighed.

Doug checked his phone. "Say, shouldn't you be getting to your mosque?"

"Yes, I should." Aziz got up. At least he could go to his store and pray there if he decided not to go to the mosque. "I'll see you tomorrow."

Tonight the breeze brought the smell of rain, and with the humidity came the amplified smells of hundreds of people. A coyote pressed a Neutra-Scent tissue to his nose as he passed Aziz, and were Aziz possessed of a long, sensitive nose, he might have been tempted to do the same. Back in Madiyah, the drier air kept smells more localized; a fennec friend of his had never complained about smells even in the middle of the busiest market.

He turned the corner, where Tanska sat behind the counter of the pastry shop, working at her register. Aziz paused at the window with the CLOSED sign in it, then walked on.

At his store, he paused again, but only for a moment. It could be that the red fox from the mosque had not heard him, and even if he had, maybe he would respect Aziz's privacy and keep it to himself. Spying was frowned upon in Islam, and most Muslims did not have Aziz's familiarity with other people's lives. In any case, for Aziz not to go to the mosque would be to appear guilty. He should go and act as though everything were normal, because it was.

He entered the mosque guardedly, but nobody paid him any special attention. He washed with the rest of them, made his way to a spot on the floor, and relaxed as the imam led them in prayer. The familiar words calmed Aziz, took him out of himself and let him focus again on his faith, his part in the world around him.

But when he got up, he noticed the red fox standing with a pangolin and a fennec, their muzzles close together and talking urgently. The fox turned to look at him and the other two followed. Aziz's fur prickled. Tail lashing, he followed his first instinct and headed for the door.

Outside, his panic subsided somewhat, replaced by regret and some anger. If only he hadn't been so careless, talking about relationships in his store where anyone might overhear. And he hadn't even done anything wrong. It was Gerald's assumption that he was gay because he'd come to a gay bar, watched a gay couple's honeymoon tape. Because he was having problems with his wife and had rejected his gay son. Because he'd let Gerald make that assumption.

(Because he'd felt comfortable talking to Gerald, because he kept picturing the tight stretch of the cougar's t-shirt over his chest.)

And that was all it was, an assumption. Even if Aziz admitted to himself that there had been something about that tape, about the way those two kissed, even about the troubles in their marriage that made him feel akin to them in some way, that didn't mean that he himself was gay. He loved his wife—or had. They'd had a cub together, and he'd always enjoyed their lovemaking.

He stopped at the street corner across from the Homeporium and looked up its walls. Blue glass reflected the stores across from it, warped but recognizable, almost artistic in the blue color palette. At the ground level, shop signs and posters set into the walls now stood as dark as the stores they were advertising. Above them, the blue glass face was broken up by patios, a few occupied; a wolf couple held wine glasses and looked out over the city, a raccoon and Dall sheep stood and talked while another sheep leaned over the railing. There was a penthouse level, but although it was lit up, Aziz saw no movement there.

The main entrance to the Homeporium was through the large open gate at the corner; from Aziz's store he could see the gate but not beyond. Here at the crosswalk, the open colorful atrium at the core of the large tower lay beyond two department stores squatting like a Scylla and Charybdis through which any visitors had to pass. The stream of people was fewer now that all the tourists had returned to their hotels, but a few, most likely residents, strolled along the red flagstones that led into the heart of the Homeporium. Aziz took a breath and crossed the street.

On the other crosswalk, the smells were different. Aziz's neighborhood had a comforting scent of all the people who lived there, the age of the buildings, exhaust of cars, the trees, and some less pleasant odors, all mixed to form a background scent that he thought of as home. Here, subtle misters set into the cornices that ran across the first story of shops breathed a soft floral scent (lavender probably; it was what everyone used, but it was faint enough that Aziz couldn't tell) that complemented the actual flowers planted in circular gardens around which the paths wound.

Aziz stepped between the large stores—those were still open, though people were leaving and nobody was entering, so likely they were closing soon. The display windows held slender female mannequins of varying colors to show how the blue dresses they wore would look on a russet fox, or a yellow leopard, or a grey wolf. He stopped to look at the leopard mannequin, envisioning the dress on Halifa. She would never wear it; it revealed too much fur and she was still modest in her tastes.

Farther into the Homeporium itself, the C-shape of its apartment towers blocked out Aziz's view of the surrounding neighborhood, but the grand interior took all his attention. A sculpture of sheltered staircases and railings whose paint wasn't chipped or worn rose around him, with shops strategically placed for easy access, fountains and benches, and brightly colored canvas roofs that remained stretched over many of the paths from the previous day's rain. Aziz felt as though he'd walked into a museum, an exhibit showing what the future was like.

He had to consult a map to find the food court patio, and then another to find out which of the stairs would take him to it. When he arrived into a cloud of frying grease and pizza smells, he found Gerald easily, sitting alone at a table. For a moment, he paused and watched.

The cougar was finishing off a burger. The curl of his arm and the swell of his bicep under the t-shirt sleeve as he lifted the last bite to his muzzle fascinated Aziz, and then his tongue licked over each finger and the cheetah's own fingers curled and twitched in response. Gerald's muzzle turned his way; Aziz, conscious that it looked like he was spying, hurried forward.

"Hey." The cougar raised his eyebrows as Aziz walked up. He picked up one of the clump of fries covered in cheese on his plate and gestured to the chair opposite him. Aziz sat, curling his tail around the chair leg out of habit. "You going to get some food?" Gerald asked. "I'll wait."

None of the cartoonish food stands around appealed to him. "I'm fine."

"Cheese fry?" Gerald pushed the tray toward him. "The places here are all wraps and salads and healthy shit. There's just the one place that makes cheese fries, but they're pretty good."

Aziz shook his head. "Thank you." He set both his paws on the table.

They looked at each other for long seconds, and then Gerald said, "So why do you care what's going on in my marriage?"

"You told me some of what was happening," Aziz replied. "But Ben obviously still loves you. That camera—that tape—" Gerald's brow lowered at the reminder. "They meant a lot to him," Aziz hurried to say.

"They do, yeah."

"But not to you."

Gerald sighed. "Not as much. Look, we had some good times. We loved each other. Who could expect that to last forever?"

"Isn't that how the vows go?" Aziz held up a paw. "Halifa and I are bound together forever, but that was back in Madiyah. My married friends here say 'until death parts us' but there is a lot of divorce, too."

"Can you not get divorced?" Gerald inclined his head.

"We can. In Islam, it is merely a matter of the husband saying to the wife, 'I divorce you,' though you have to say it three times for it to be final. It's called *talāq*. Couples who feel the need to divorce are encouraged to attempt to reconcile before finalizing it, though."

"And you haven't yet?"

Aziz's back began to ache. He stretched and then relaxed it. "We aren't unhappy exactly. We live our separate lives and sleep in the same house and share ownership of the business. It isn't worth the energy to divorce."

"What would be worth the energy?"

"Well…" Aziz hesitated. "Adultery is a terrible sin. So if one of us felt attraction outside the marriage—no, more. If one of us wanted to start a relationship with someone else, then we would probably ask the other for divorce to pursue it. But that would mean complicating the business, the house…" He trailed off, thinking of the beach in Coronado. "I don't know that another relationship would be worthwhile. Can we fall in love again this late in life?"

"Of course you can." Gerald's ears perked. "Sure. My mom and dad split twenty years ago and mom just got remarried a couple years back. She's really happy with this new guy, too."

"Thank you for reminding me I'm old enough to be your father."

Gerald laughed. "Why does that matter?"

"I don't feel like your elder. I feel like we're going through the same thing, only I have almost thirty years of marriage behind me instead of three." Aziz exhaled and stared down at his paws. "It's harder to throw that away."

"You're not throwing it away, though." Gerald leaned forward. "How you feel now doesn't invalidate what you used to have. That's what I keep trying to tell Ben. He thinks that we were in love once and so we should always be, and if we're not it's because one of us did something wrong. And he blames himself, of course, because he loves me." The cougar's voice acquired a soft growl. "I keep telling him that we changed, it's nobody's fault. He doesn't care, doesn't want to listen. Love is pure and good and all that."

"Love is good," Aziz said.

"Sure, but…you can't force it."

"But you can work for it. That's what I feel." He looked up to the night sky, city light reflected off clouds, the light of the moon nowhere to be seen. "That if I'd worked harder, maybe tried more to be involved in her activities, maybe we wouldn't have drifted apart."

"Or she could've tried to be interested in your activities," Gerald said.

"She was, at first. She's the one who reached out for more things. I was happy to keep my life as it was. She's going out and finding causes to champion, new adventures…I only wanted to keep my store."

Gerald nodded, licked cheese from his fingers, and then said, "Look, if I'm out of line, I'm sorry, but…if you're gay and you were never attracted to her, that can be hard."

"I'm not." The words emerged automatically and fell cold and flat to the metal table.

The cougar raised his eyebrows. "You're not gay? I mean, bi maybe, but the way you've been looking at me, the way you were talking…"

Aziz shook his head. "My apologies. I shouldn't have snapped. What I mean is…attraction was never an issue. I loved her. We have a cub."

Gerald smiled. "Hell, I've slept with females too. It didn't excite me, and more, I never felt the connection with any of them that I felt with Ben. Being gay doesn't mean you hate females, or throw up if you see one naked or something. It means that when you feel that spark, it'll most likely be with a guy. So maybe you are bi. Bisexual, that is. I know with your religion it's hard, but it's a fact of biology. Whatever god you believe in made you that way."

"I'm not, though—I mean, I don't know if—" Aziz exhaled. "Islam doesn't condemn anyone for feeling attraction to the same sex. They condemn for acting on it. But in many of the stories of Islam, gay people are known—it's actually supposed to be a dangerous temptation in many of our stories, believe it or not."

"But you don't see it that way?"

He heard again the chanting of the crowd, the dimly familiar cheetah on the rooftop, the terror in his young stomach. "I learned other lessons when I was young. There are many different Islamic societies all around the world, and mine was…" He sighed and shifted in his chair to ease the weight on his back. "It's just not possible to be gay and Muslim in many places now. Most places." Here, though, in Port City in the twenty-first century?

"Yeah. Ben grew up in a Catholic family and he found a lot of stories about the Catholic church blessing relationships between same sex partners in the Middle Ages or something. Didn't cut a lot of mustard with his family at first. They're cool with him now, but what did it was him, not some stories about the church."

"Does he still go to church?"

"Uh." Gerald shook his head. "No. Neither of us do."

"I go every day. I just came from my mosque."

The cougar sat back in his chair and looked around. A few of the fast food places were rolling down grates over their windows, and only a well-dressed fox couple shared the patio with them, several tables away. "If your religion isn't letting you be who you really are…"

"I've told you, that's not the problem."

Gerald sighed. "Look, I had this bro in the army, he was the same way. He was married to his high school sweetheart, he swore up and down that he was straight. But when he'd talk about her, he was never like, 'she's so sexy,' unless the other guys were talking about their girlfriends. Then he'd latch onto whatever they were talking about. Like if Andy was talking about his girlfriend's tits and how much he liked getting his paws on them, this friend of mine would say his girlfriend had really nice tits too. But it was never—it was never how much *he* enjoyed it, you know?"

"I'm not really comfortable with this vulgar talk," Aziz said, because he was also annoyed that Gerald was presuming to know him.

"Sorry. But you see what I'm saying?"

"I don't see how it relates. I told you attraction wasn't an issue."

"Right." Gerald dabbed one of his last fries at a rapidly congealing pile of cheese. "You're also not trying to impress a bunch of horny early twenties guys. You're mature enough to recognize that part. My buddy, though, when he found out I was gay—I was pretty open—he was a jackass about it for a while. Like, asking me all the time if I missed sucking—uh, if I missed oral sex. Asking if such-and-such guy was 'hot' to me. Saying he didn't get how a guy could find love under another guy's tail. Like, way more explicit stuff than he ever said about his girlfriend."

Aziz folded his arms. "He was gay, is what you're saying."

"I think so. I mean, we got really drunk together when we got back Stateside before he headed back to Pensa, and he told me that the whole time we were out there, he wanted to ask me if he could suck—sorry. You know."

"I get it." Aziz waved a paw, trying not to betray the uneasy stirrings of desire the language and images were provoking in him.

"I told him I was married and I wouldn't have let him. He wasn't my type anyway—I like predators. But he kept saying I was so lucky to have someone to do that, and then he told me that he and his best friend in high school used to fool around until his friend wanted to make it more serious and he told the guy to fuck off—sorry—because he wasn't gay."

"Charming."

"Yeah. But he wished he could have someone like that again. Someone he got rid of by his own choice." The fox couple rose to leave. Gerald glanced over and extended his paws out on the table, taking a breath and letting it out slowly. "Anyway. The point is that he had a lot of reasons not to admit that he was gay, but it didn't change the fact."

Aziz cleared his throat. Gerald had believed that he was gay when they met at Founders, a lie of omission that Aziz had allowed to continue. What if that lie had been a truth hidden so deeply that Aziz himself had not been able to feel it until another pointed it out to him? They were alone now on the patio, him and Gerald, and there would be nobody else to hear his confession. He stared at the cougar and tried to imagine for a moment that his fascination was in fact physical attraction, that this handsome, muscular soldier was as desirable to him as his wife had once been, years ago.

Dangerous, he thought, his heart speeding up. *Not allowed. Wrong.* But that wasn't the question; the question was whether he *wanted* it. "What I feel isn't material," he said both to Gerald and himself. "I can't act on it."

"So you're trying to fix my marriage as a sort of proxy?" Gerald didn't wait for an answer, but leaned forward. His voice dropped to a whisper. "When you watched that video, did you wish it was you?"

The cougar stared into his eyes and Aziz couldn't look away. "Did you wish it was you with Ben? Or with me? Whatever you imagined us doing after you shut it off…do you want me to do that to you?"

The stirrings became full-on churnings in his gut, the heat lower. Aziz kept his eyes steady and his paws on the table. "I told you, I'm married."

"Okay, then, not any of the sex stuff. Just to hold you, to look into your eyes that way."

The "yes" caught in his throat. He swallowed. "We are both married with vows to keep."

Gerald's eyes didn't look away, but the cougar smiled and leaned back. "I'm only trying to help. The sooner you admit to yourself that this is what you want, the easier it'll be. It won't be me, but maybe you can divorce your wife and find a companion you'll enjoy spending the next few decades with instead of being bound to a promise you made years ago."

Recovering a little of his composure, Aziz leaned forward. "Are you sure you aren't coaxing me to leave my marriage so you'll feel better about leaving yours?"

The cougar's smile vanished. He opened his mouth and then closed it again. Aziz went on. "I have experience, too. I have seen divorce, and have a friend who had already made up her mind to leave her husband. This was years ago. For months before the divorce, she asked 'hypothetical' questions of everyone: if you made a promise years ago but the circumstances around the promise change, do you have to keep it? If two people agreed to keep a garden together but one decided that she didn't like gardening anymore, did the other have to do his share as well? You talk divorce very casually, but it is a weighty thing, to throw away this promise."

"I'm not 'throwing it away.' I'm…I'm not sure it applies anymore."

"Do you know why we have a strict prohibition against adultery?"

"Because marriage is God's law, I guess."

"It is a legal binding. The prohibition against adultery is because it is an 'evil deed,' that's what the Qu'ran says about it. It's breaking a promise, a vow, and in so doing you allow yourself to break other vows. It's not because it will anger your god or anything like that. It's because the promises you make are important, and keeping them is important, and if you choose to end a promise, you should think about it and actually make an end to it, rather than just stopping because you don't feel the same as you did three years ago."

Gerald's ears lowered. "So I should have to keep this promise even though we've both changed?"

"You have both changed," Aziz said. "Who's to say you might not change back?"

"Is that what you hope? That your feelings will go away and you can go back to your business arrangement of a marriage?"

"I don't know what I hope. I only know that things are changing all around me." Aziz looked up at the glass towers with their bright concrete patios. "And so I can't stay the same. But do I go with my wife or try to find my own way? And if you're right about me, then my dissatisfaction is the result of feelings I can't act on, so why not stay with a wife who is pleased with our 'business arrangement,' as you put it?"

"Your faith is the problem, not your wife. Why not go ahead and be yourself? Most of my friends who grew up Christian don't go to church anymore. Any god that would make you a certain way and then forbid you to act on the way he made you doesn't deserve your faith anyway."

Aziz shook his head. "That's nonsensical." He stopped himself. "I'm sorry. My faith is part of my world. That would be like…telling someone to cure their pollen allergy by ceasing to breathe. I can't ignore or give up my beliefs."

Gerald held up a finger. "But you said your son did. Have you talked to him about your feelings?"

"No."

"You should. Maybe he'd have some insight."

"He's given up his faith completely," Aziz said.

"But you still talk to him." The cougar raised his eyebrows.

A breeze swirled through the atrium, ruffling Aziz's fur. "To be honest," he said slowly, "it is my wife who talks to him. I suspect. She has not admitted it."

"You're the one who cut him off." Gerald did not seem surprised by this information. When Aziz nodded, the cougar smiled very slightly. "And now you're in the same position he was in. You feel now how hard it must have been for him?"

"No," Aziz snapped. "Because he never took his faith seriously. Here in the States, faith is not so important. Like you and your husband, like 'most everyone you know,' this country values the individual more than the spiritual."

"It's not that we don't value the spiritual."

Aziz cut Gerald off. "This focus on the individual means that this is a country of individuals. Nobody feels any duty to anyone else. And I'm holding on to my faith because I am letting go in other areas. Look: I own a store and these people," his paw gestured up at the towers around them, "are coming in to tear down our stores and our neighborhood, and I and all the other store owners are letting them do it. Why? Because they are paying us a lot of money. It is a good business decision, which means it is good for my wife and me. Individual gain. So I'm holding on to my faith, the one part of my life where I do think of others and I do think of my community, and now…" He remembered the fox in the mosque. "Now even that is threatened. Maybe."

"You haven't told anyone, have you?" Gerald tilted his head. "You barely told me."

"Someone overheard." Aziz cut himself off. No need to make Gerald feel bad about talking to him in his shop. "Or saw me. At the bar, I mean."

"Oh." Gerald rubbed his whiskers. "Sorry about that, again."

Aziz shook his head. "Think nothing of it. I lied to you…several times. I'm not proud of that."

"It's scary." Gerald slumped back in his chair.

The cheetah nodded. "So is ending a marriage."

"Well, not as scary as the truck at the front of your convoy getting blown up." Gerald stared down at the table. "I guess, not as immediately life-threatening."

"But you're creating the fear," Aziz said. "Not reacting to it. Reacting is easier because you don't have to make decisions."

"True." Gerald smiled. "Hey, you still need to eat. Want to go somewhere that isn't here? I hadn't realized how you felt about this place taking over the neighborhood."

Aziz shook his head. "We have food at home. I will probably eat there. And I should talk to my wife—about our son, if nothing else."

"All right. Hey, let me give you my number. If you want to talk again, just text me. I'm usually free in the evenings."

"Of course." Aziz took out his phone and they exchanged numbers.

While Gerald took his trash to the bin, Aziz stood and examined the towers and the shopping plaza around him. Most of the stores and kiosks were closed now, and few people roamed the intricate stairs and walkways of the mall. But above them more people sat out on their patios, enjoying the cool spring night, and if he tuned out the piped-in music of the shopping center, he could catch murmurs of conversation drifting down to him. He put a paw to his back, but the ache there had diminished and was barely noticeable now.

"Heading out?" Gerald followed his gaze up to the apartments. "Yeah, those are really something, eh? I thought they looked weird in this neighborhood. Really didn't like them at first, but I'm getting used to them."

"You know about Port City belonging to the squirrel tribe, I think it was?" Aziz fell into step with the cougar toward one of the stairs.

"Yeah, the main island." Gerald gestured in the general direction of the cluster of skyscrapers that marked Port Island at the center of the metropolis, hidden now behind blue glass and concrete.

"It seems to me that this is somewhat the same thing that is going on now. The Vorvarts people are buying the land from those who hold title to it to move in their own settlers." He looked up again at the apartments. Here inside the structure, they only reflected each other. "It's not fair to the people who are moving out, but the people moving in are people, too. We all have to live somewhere."

Gerald nodded. "I've only lived here less than a year, but all the old people talking about how this is ruining the neighborhood—I don't see it. I guess the argument is, these people can afford to live anywhere, so why do they have to take the homes of people who've lived here for decades? But nothing lasts forever, does it?" He snorted. "There's people talking about Times Square and how much better it was when it smelled like piss and was full of X-rated bookstores. But you know what? I like being able to go there at night without a big knife to defend myself."

"We moved here after it was full of junkies, but we don't go now that it's full of tourists." Aziz looked around as they passed chain store after chain store. "I don't have any particular dislike for these stores, but I'd never shop here."

"I would, when we have money." Gerald waved a paw toward one of them. "J. Kewn has pretty good clothes. But there's a nicer one over in Cottage Hill."

"I'm sure." Aziz glanced at Gerald's t-shirt and camo pants.

"When we have money, I said." The cougar scowled, then the scowl melted into a smile. "Do you just get your clothes from what people don't buy at your store?"

"No. But we don't shop often." Aziz paused at the cougar's expression. "Was that supposed to be an insult?"

"No. Well, I mean." Gerald gestured. "A friendly jab. Like your look at my clothes."

Aziz allowed himself a smile. "I was wondering whether you considered those clothes 'pretty good.'"

"There you go," Gerald said. "All right, now we're going back and forth, we're both kinda shitty dressers. Does your wife nag you about your clothes?"

"Not usually." Aziz's mind turned to Halifa, and what he would say to her tonight. They hadn't properly talked since the meeting, and now he thought they would have to, soon.

"Ben gave up a couple months ago. He used to try to get me to some of those fancier stores, but that one," the cougar jerked his thumb back toward the J. Kewn store, "is about as fancy as I can stomach. Just different tastes."

"Indeed." They walked between the two large stores, and the cool, clean air of the Homeporium fell away from them.

"Well…good luck." Gerald extended a paw, and Aziz clasped it.

"You too," the cheetah said. "And thank you for taking the time to talk."

"Ah." Gerald waved his paw. "I don't have many people to talk to about this stuff. Most of my friends are all like, 'save the marriage,' and nobody actually listens to what's going on."

"It's hard to find people to listen sometimes," Aziz agreed. "Let me know how it goes."

"Sure." Gerald started to walk away, then half-turned and said, "After all, you've seen our tape. You're practically family."

Aziz's ears flattened. "Is that another 'friendly jab'?"

"More or less." Gerald grinned and made to turn away.

"I told you, I didn't watch all of the tape," Aziz said abruptly.

Gerald's hazel eyes, dark in the evening, measured him. "The kiss was still pretty intimate. I mean, it's not as racy as what came after, but you're still one of only three people who's seen that."

Aziz again imagined what might've come after the kiss on the tape. Gerald's paw waving in front of his eyes broke the reverie. "Hey," the cougar said. "If we get close, someday I might tell you what we did."

"It's all right," the cheetah said hastily, ears flattening. "I should not have watched any of it."

"I'm teasing you," Gerald said. He laid a paw on Aziz's shoulder, as warm as his smile. "See you 'round." And then he waved and disappeared into the crowd.

Chapter Twelve: A Door Opens

His path home took him past the shop, and he stopped there, putting a paw up on the cracked wood of the door frame. "Character," his customers called it, but to Aziz it looked worn and old. Twenty years ago, it had still been old, but he and Halifa had worked to sand the wood and paint it themselves, to save a little of the money that was going to the contractors who replaced the warped floorboards and the stained walls inside the shop. And now, over the years, the wood had been warped again by age, the walls stained by use.

They'd talked a few years ago about renovating the store if the Homeporium did poorly. But that talk had faded right around the time Marquize had left for good, and now there was no more point to it. His claw dug into one of the cracks, pulled the wood apart. It would have been nice to renovate, or even to allow some young entrepreneur to buy the property, to sand down Aziz and Halifa's old paint job with his wife and repaint it, to turn it into a cupcake shop or a dress boutique or something.

Or even, Aziz thought, for an entrepreneur and his husband. Or an entrepreneur and her wife. The world was so different now from when he and Halifa had come here and started their lives, and yet in many ways it was the same. People feared change; people clung to each other; people forged ahead and changed the world.

He looked through the glass at the interior of the shop, at all the items people had shed from their past lives. Then he walked on down the block.

At the corner, workers were beginning to cover the Space Wolf billboard over the café Casablanca. The café was closed; the patio was empty. Aziz touched the metal railing and then walked with the sparser crowd of people back toward his home.

Halifa sat in the living room. The TV was on to the evening news, but she was looking at her phone, ignoring the screen. "Good evening," she said as Aziz entered the house.

He closed the front door behind him and walked down the short hall to the living room. They had found a Madiyan rug a decade or more ago, with a simple pattern of blue, orange, and green stripes. The comfortable loveseat on which Halifa sat was States-made, brown velvet, and the matching armchair was empty, but Aziz chose to sit cross-legged on the rug. "Evening," he said.

"It seemed as though we should talk." She put down her phone.

"I think so, too."

Their eyes met, and then she slid down off the couch to sit on the floor a few feet from him. She pulled the scarf from her head to rest around her neck. "Are you going to try to talk me out of selling?"

Aziz shook his head. "There's no reason not to sell. No real one."

"Mm." She tilted her head. "Tanska is okay with this?"

"Tanska doesn't own our store."

"Fair enough." Halifa spread her paws. "And then?"

"After the sale?" She nodded. Aziz rubbed at his whiskers. "Doug is moving to Coronado. He invited us along."

Halifa's ears perked. "Both of us? Hm. I don't know that I wish to move across the country."

"I didn't think you would."

"I have my work here, and my friends."

Aziz nodded. They looked at each other and then away, and he curled his tail around his legs. "What if I were to move there?"

"Without me?" She didn't seem at all bothered by the idea, but considered it carefully, as though he'd suggested purchasing a new property for the business. "Do you think you'd like it in Coronado?"

"There are mosques there, but not as many as here. There's beaches and sun, and Doug would be out there. He's the only friend I have left here." Although Gerald had engaged in "friendly jabs"; did that mean they were friends?

"You've never complained about the weather."

"No. I don't mind it." He rested his paws on his ankles and thought about Coronado, the pictures he'd seen and the idea of living far away from everyone. Just him and Doug for another twenty or thirty years. "What would I do if I stayed here?"

"You're not interested in my charities. You're not interested in Tanska's neighborhood. What would you like to do?"

She gestured to him, her paw open. Aziz reached out and touched his fingertips to hers. He looked at the black pads at the end of his golden-furred fingertips, her black pads and golden-furred fingers like a mirror image. "I don't know. Maybe that's the problem. My old life is coming apart piece by piece and I have nothing to put in its place."

"Aziz." At his name, he looked up and into her eyes. "We left behind one old life. We can leave behind another. You can continue to manage the stores, move to a different neighborhood perhaps."

Managing the other stores felt to him like the Space Wolf movie: trying to recapture a feeling from his youth. He wasn't sure that would satisfy him anymore. Halifa saw that in his eyes and went on. "Or you find something to do in Coronado. Work with the mosques there. They're always happy to have more people involved." She paused. "You could visit your son."

Aziz's brow lowered and he took his paw back from hers. "You have been talking to him."

"Yes. I know you asked me not to, but I don't think that's for the best. He's living on the West Coast, not in Coronado but a few hours north of there, I believe." She paused. "He's doing well."

Aziz drew his knees up. "I have no interest in his life."

"That notwithstanding, he has a life. He has a boyfriend. He has a job teaching tennis to young people at an athletic club." She steepled her fingers together when Aziz did not reply. "If you do nothing else in your life, you have to repair the breach between you."

"It's not a breach," Aziz said. "It's a chasm. He stood in this house and said that our faith was worthless, that his feelings were stronger than the teachings we live by."

"They need not be mutually exclusive." Halifa looked over her fingertips at him.

Did she know? Aziz felt a guilty pang in his stomach, thinking back to the conversation he'd come from. But even if he did feel those same feelings, he kept them in check because they were not part of his world. "There are Muslims who drink, too," he said. "That is not how I practice."

"Have you in fact examined the Qu'ran, the hadiths, the teachings of the rightly-guided caliphs?"

"Of course I've read them." Aziz tilted his head. He and Halifa had talked little about their religion in the early years of their marriage, more when they had arrived in the States and were trying to teach their son.

"Recently?" He said nothing. Halifa nodded. "I have gone back to them to try to understand our son."

"Our son wants nothing to do with our faith, our teachings, our beliefs." Aziz's tail tip flicked.

"No. But if we wish to include him in our world, then we must understand what our faith truly says about him."

"Include him in our world?" Aziz rose to his feet in a fluid motion, his tail lashing now. "Why should we? Has he expressed any wish to be included in it?"

"Because we are his parents and he is our son."

"A relationship which he disavowed right here!" Aziz pointed to the carpet and then the door. "Have you gone back to that conversation as well, to understand him?"

Halifa remained seated. "You and he were both angry. You both said things you did not mean."

"I meant every word. And so, I believe, did he." He stalked back and forth across the floor.

His wife looked up at him with a tolerant smile. "We're cheetahs, all of us. We move quickly and speak quickly, and often we say things that would be better held back and considered. 'When you become angry, keep silent.'"

He scowled at the Qu'ran quotation, but bowed his head. "I have not always behaved my best. Why bring this up now?"

Now Halifa rose. "Because we are at a turning point in our lives. I believe that you and I may part ways with the sale of this store and the changing of this block."

Aziz stopped, even his tail, and looked at her. She stood a little shorter than he, with a simple yellow dress and the brown-bordered scarf around her neck. Her fur, a darker gold than his, contrasted well with the dress. He saw her in that moment not merely as his wife, but as a lovely, independent cheetah with her own life, doing good where she saw the opportunity. He felt a rush of unworthiness. "'May'?" he said softly. "Is that what you want?"

"Is it not what you want?" she countered, and he bowed his head.

"I'm sorry," she went on, "that it took this long for me to speak my mind, that I waited. It was easier not to cause trouble, and both of you were so angry. I should have tried to reconcile you before now."

"No," Aziz said, not because it was untrue but because he didn't want her to bear the blame. "We would not have talked. Might not even now."

"You will eventually. The wounds are not as raw as they were three years ago, are they?"

"The scars are still there." His claws raked down his arm, parting the fur and stinging his skin.

"We can live with scars. I'm not saying you should forgive him for the things he said, nor that he should forgive you for the things you said." She held up a paw to still his protest. "I'm saying that those things are in the past. We can move forward from them."

"The Qu'ran, the hadiths, those are all part of the past, too," he said, and then recalled her quotation and softened his tone. "Should we move on from them as well?"

"Now you're just being argumentative," she said.

"Not at all." He faced her across the rug. "You want to keep the parts of the past that you like and throw away the parts you don't. But you don't get that choice. The world changes and moves on, and you can only keep what you can hold onto yourself. The things we hold onto from the past define how we move forward."

"Then why are you holding on to this anger against Marquize?" He flattened his ears at the name, as though she'd summoned his spirit. If she noticed, she ignored it. "I know what happened to your uncle. It was terrible and tragic, and you should not have been made to watch it. That also is a scar you carry with you—one you choose to carry with you."

"Choose?" The word burst out, Qu'ranic proscriptions forgotten. "You think I choose to have that memory? I would do anything I could not to see it again!"

"You choose to carry it. You let it define how you treated your son. You view it as part of the world instead of part of the culture in which we grew up, a culture we left behind. We live in a new place, with new customs, and that part of our lives is over, Aziz. Now we are moving again, and again you have a chance to change."

It isn't that easy, he wanted to yell, but this time he stilled his words before they could emerge. If he took her advice, if he thought through their situation, then what conclusion would he come to? Had he simply been accepting that part of his life and his history for all these years, not approaching it from a new perspective?

His uncle, his son—both were gone, but one was not beyond his reach. And what of himself in all this? If he reached out to his son, would he gain some understanding of himself and thereby some peace? He'd thought that simply living according to shari'a law, acknowledging his desires without acting on them, would be enough for him. But if he could accept his son's actions…

One thing at a time. He exhaled and stepped forward to take Halifa's paw. "If I wanted to read what you have been reading," he said, "where would I start?"

Chapter Thirteen: Semantic Reading

Armed with Halifa's readings, Aziz returned to the Devos Musjid Al-Islam the following evening. If anyone challenged him, he could say he was reading the scriptures to resolve some personal issues.

At the door, he paused. He could go pray in his store. But to run away from his community…that was what Marquize had done. He could prove he was stronger. So he pushed open the door and walked in.

Nobody challenged him. Those who met his eyes smiled and nodded in greeting. He didn't see the red fox at first, not until he had already washed and was kneeling for prayer. And then he lost himself in in the familiar, welcome words, reminding himself that he was part of the world just as everyone else, and that everyone had desires to fight and challenges to meet.

Afterwards, everything was as it had been. Aziz stood with the rest of the males, some talking, some examining the community board. The red fox was talking to two others, but not looking at Aziz, and then he broke away, and Aziz, on impulse, moved to intercept him.

"Oh," the fox said when he saw Aziz. "Salaam."

"Salaam." Aziz took a breath. "You were in my shop yesterday."

"Yes. You gave me a fair price." The fox wouldn't meet his eyes. "Is there a problem?"

"Whatever you might have…overheard," Aziz forced the words out. "Is my personal business. I'm reading scripture and searching for answers myself. Nobody else needs to know."

At that, the fox looked up and his eyes widened. "Sir," he said, "I would not presume…"

"You were looking at me," Aziz said before he could think to leave the situation alone. "And talking to a pangolin and another."

"I was telling them about your store." The fox gave an earnest smile. "Recommending they give you their business. I didn't say anything about what," he flicked his ears, "I might have heard."

"Oh." Aziz's ears flushed, and he bowed his head. "Please accept my apologies."

"No, no!" The fox reached out and took his paw. "I understand how it must have looked. I wasn't sure how to handle it."

"My name is Aziz." Aziz turned the grasp into a formal clasping of paws.

"Marris."

"Thank you very much for your referral."

Aziz released the fox's paw and turned to go, but the fox hurried up alongside him. "Would you step outside a moment?"

The cheetah eyed Marris warily, and then nodded and followed him out.

Others already stood on the sidewalk outside checking their phones in the warm Port City night. Marris took his out and gestured for Aziz to step a bit away from the crowd. "If you are reading scripture and you have questions, I know a group that might help."

"A group?"

"For people with questions about sexuality." The fox held his phone up and Aziz saw an address listed on it. "They're open to anyone with questions. I'm sure Mr. Samara would love to talk to you."

Warning signs forty years old flickered in Aziz's head. He looked around, but nobody was paying attention to them, nobody was watching to see whether he would accept the offer. He copied the address down quickly. "Are you...?"

"No, not me. But my sister had questions last year in college. She said they were very helpful. She still meets with them."

Aziz stared at the street name on his phone. "I don't know."

Marris put an encouraging paw on his arm. "Times are changing," he said. "You could still come to the Musjid here."

"If it survives the changes."

"As long as we are here, it will survive." Marris smiled. "And when we are not here, it will be wherever we are."

الْوَقْتِ الَّذِيْ يُرِيْدُ

The address was deep in Cottage Hill, a half-mile past Founders, nearly to the other side of the neighborhood. Aziz walked past rainbow-flagged store windows and same-sex couples holding paws, but otherwise he would not have been able to tell that this was a gay community. The stores, small and bustling with cheerful clientele and clerks, looked very similar to the way he remembered Nassau Street in decades past.

Summer would not officially arrive for almost another month, but the streets steamed under the hot sun and it felt like the first day of the Port City summer. Bare chests and short skirts abounded, with sunglasses and one or two parasols to protect sensitive ears. Aziz liked the feel of the hot sun on his ears and kept them up as he strode through the crowds of people out in the streets.

He'd worn a nice collared shirt, not as nice as the one he and Halifa had worn to the bank the previous day, but nice enough that he looked like a tourist in the busy Cottage Hill neighborhood, especially when he took his phone out to check the directions. But he didn't stop in any of the shops with signs up that showed where they'd been featured on TV, nor did he pause at the historic 1913 school building.

Ficus Street climbed the side of a gentle hill, and 299 was near the top. Aziz pushed his way up the pavement, panting slightly in the warm, humid air, and found himself in front of a two-story row house painted purple. There were no signs on it nor any indication that it was anything other than a residence, so Aziz checked the address again, and yes, that was right.

At the door, he found the name "SAMARA" on the listing and pressed the doorbell for it. A moment later, a short lion—young, his mane just coming in—answered the door. Aziz frowned. "Mr. Samara?"

"That's right. I'm Bakr. You're—oh, Aziz?"

"Aziz Alhazhari, yes."

"Oh, come in, come in!" Aziz followed the lion in and saw as he approached that the mane was not in fact coming in, but had been shaved down to a half-inch or so.

Bakr showed him into a small room with a Persian rug next to a fine polished coffee table bearing an ornate silver tea service, surrounded by a green couch and pair of armchairs with shiny worn patches on the arms. Around the room were landscapes of sand dunes and a family portrait of six lions of varying ages, as well as a delicately-crafted birdcage painted white, hanging from the ceiling, and a fireplace that smelled lightly of wood smoke.

"Does the smoke bother you?" Bakr said anxiously. "I can light incense."

"No, I'm fine, thank you." Aziz rested a paw on the green armchair closest to him.

"Please, have a seat. Tea?"

The mint smell overwhelmed everything else once he sat in the chair. "Please."

Bakr poured out two cups and then sat. "So, you said in the e-mail that you have a gay son…?"

"Yes."

The lion waited politely for a moment and then said, "Sometimes it's easier if I start by talking about the group here, and then you can talk to me about anything you like." Aziz nodded, and the lion settled back. "Officially we're the Cottage Hill Muslim Society, but online we're Queer Muslims of Cottage Hill. I keep wanting to make us Queer Muslims of Port City, but everyone says there are other groups, even though none of them is really well organized. Anyway. The point is, we're not a mosque or anything, though we do pray together often. We're a support group and a discussion group. We talk about the words of the prophet, peace be upon him, and we talk about our homosexual experience within our faith. We don't have any parents of gay Muslims, but I want to make sure we're welcoming to all."

"Peace be upon him," Aziz murmured in response. When Bakr looked expectantly at him, he said, "My son...three years ago he walked out of our house. He said he was gay, and we'd known that, but I had told him that the Qu'ran instructs us to accept the urges and never act on them." He sighed. "But Marquize was always wilful, and Islam never meant to him what it does to me and his mother. He told me that our faith was an archaic remnant of an ancient civilization, used all over the world to oppress freedom and hurt people."

"Ah." Bakr nodded. "We hear that a lot, but usually from outsiders."

"And," Aziz went on, "he told us that he'd been acting on his urges. That he had a boyfriend and had been engaging in...in relations with him."

"That must have been very hard."

"It was. I didn't handle it very well."

Bakr sipped his tea. "For him as well, I mean."

"What?"

"To tell you, his father, whom he respects more than anyone in the world, that he's betrayed such an important element of your faith? To lash out at your faith, something so important to you? He must have been very frustrated."

Aziz breathed in the smell of mint, his irritation growing. Perhaps this had been a mistake. "He never respected our faith."

The lion inclined his head. "It sounds as though he was using your faith as the sharpest weapon he could. People lash out when they're afraid; the worse the lash, the greater their fear."

"That doesn't change the fact of what he said."

"No, but it helps you understand why he said it."

"I know why he said it!" Aziz's paw trembled; he set the tea cup down. "He's always resented our faith. Never wanted to be a part of it."

"Maybe that's because he felt rejected by it."

"How could he? He never gave it a chance!"

Bakr nodded. "Did you ever ask him how early he felt these 'urges'? Ever talk to him about them, or seek answers in Islam for them?"

Aziz shook his head, slowly. The lion sipped his tea again and then set down his cup as well. "Let me tell you my story. I knew I was gay from the age of thirteen. I also knew that most of those who practice my faith wouldn't allow me to be myself in it. Like your son, perhaps, I thought at first that I could be myself simply by refraining from acting on my desires. But as I grew older, I felt that that contradiction was not consistent with the fundamental philosophy of Islam. So I studied modern works. There are people who believe that the stories used to condemn homosexuality have alternate meanings, that it may have a place in Islam. After all…" He spread his paws and smiled. "It's love, is it not?"

"It's lust. Desire." But even as he spoke the automatic response, he remembered the tape, the embrace between Benjamin and Gerald.

The lion's eyes softened. "It's more than that, Mr. Alhazhari. It's our identity. It's a connection between two souls." He curled the fingers of one paw over those of the other. "The purpose of our making is to find joy in the way our Creator made us."

"The Qur'an says these desires are to be ignored." He felt stupid saying that over and over, as though it were a rock he clung to on a cliff while the lion extended a paw to help him up.

Bakr tilted his head curiously. "It doesn't actually say that. I have a book you can read that goes into exactly what the Qur'an and the hadiths say. There are many readings, and some people use their readings to justify persecution of homosexuals. But there are other readings, and if you read the books with love in your heart then you can find love in those scriptures as well."

Anger rose again, but Aziz quelled it. He was a guest in this lion's house. "That seems facile. You can't just read scripture to get the answer you want from it."

"No, of course not. But that applies to both sides. Here's an example. In the story of the Prophet Lut, peace be upon him, the people of Sodom are punished for their transgressions." Bakr held up a paw. "They wanted to rape the angels disguised as men. Some people say that their transgression is homosexuality. But a scholar has written that the transgression is their aggressive, violent nature. Do you see how it could be read either way?"

"The word 'sodomy' in English comes from that story."

"A Christian derivation." Bakr smiled.

Aziz stopped and shook his head. "It still feels like you're making up justifications to do what you want to do."

"I'm studying a holy text to determine how to be the best person. Isn't that what our religion is about?"

Bakr's smile felt sincere and warm. Aziz's fingers curled in on themselves, tightening. He forced them to relax and open. "There are rules to follow."

"Of course. But not everyone agrees on them. Love, though; don't you think that's worth it?"

He was twelve again, standing in a hot, smelly crowd of people jumping and cheering. "My uncle." His breath came ragged. "Back in Madiyah. They threw him off a roof."

Bakr's smile vanished. He reached out a paw, then drew it back. "I'm so sorry."

The crowd around him chanting. His own dread, wondering why he didn't feel the same joy they did, trying with all his will to view his uncle as a sinner, his death a good thing. "My father took me. He made me watch."

"Your uncle was gay?"

"No!" The word exploded from him. "No! He had a friend—the son of Umar Surur, an important minister. The son, *he* was—he was homosexual. He seduced my uncle—made my uncle touch him." His imagination had supplied all kinds of vivid details at the time. "But my uncle wasn't—he was married, he loved his wife. He was killed as an *example*. As a warning to—" To the twelve-year-old who had begun to notice the bodies of the boys around him. "To all of us."

The lion bowed his head. "That's horrible."

"And you're saying—you're saying he died for nothing. That all those people who believed he was a sinner, who believed they were doing the right thing, who raised me, who gave me and Halifa money to come to this new country and helped us start a new life, that they were all wrong?"

Bakr looked steadily at him. "Forgive me," he said slowly, "but do you think they were *right*?"

It was a strange sensation, feeling the buried doubts surface after forty years. Grief and regret swelled in his chest and throat. "I—" He brought his paws to his muzzle.

"You were young." It was almost a question. Aziz didn't contest it nor respond, and Bakr went on. "You accepted what was presented to you. Those laws, those demonstrations, they were all to push someone else's reading of scripture onto you before you had a chance to read yourself and form your own opinions."

Still he couldn't speak. Bakr rose and returned with a small box of tissues, which he set on the table. That gesture, as kind and hospitable as it was, allowed Aziz to regain some measure of control. "I'm not going to cry," he said stiffly.

"This was just in case." The lion smiled. "I have talked to many people in your situation, having to rethink and reconsider the beliefs they thought were a solid foundation of their world."

Aziz shook his head. "I can't turn back to when I thought it was horrible and cruel rather than just. Those tracks are old and worn."

"Of course not. But you can change a little at a time, bit by bit. The future contains both the past and the present, as much as you allow it. And your son is still alive, so perhaps you can start by forgiving him. A small amount."

"I don't know." Aziz clasped his paws together. The smell of the mint tea calmed him, made the words easier. "But at least perhaps I see the path toward forgiveness."

Bakr nodded. "And then perhaps you may forgive yourself." Aziz jerked his head up. The lion smiled. "At least for your treatment of your son. And… forgive me if I overstep, but many who come to see me about others also have questions about…themselves?"

Aziz started to say "No," but found himself unwilling to lie. "Perhaps," he said.

"It can be very difficult to see your son giving in to the urges it has cost you so much to restrain. Having invested so much in denying yourself, it can be even more difficult to turn and give in. It will feel wrong. It won't be easy, but is not forgiveness and repentance part of the teaching of Allah and of the Prophet, peace be upon him? That forgiveness extends also to yourself."

"The future contains the past, though," Aziz said. "As you said. I can't erase that."

"But it also contains the present." Bakr gestured toward his teapot. "You might not drink heated water by itself, but add mint leaves to it and it becomes palatable. And the heat diminishes with time, if you add no more to it."

Aziz stared down at his teacup and didn't say anything. "Would you like more tea?" Bakr asked.

"No, thank you. You've been very hospitable." Aziz breathed in and sat straighter, uncurling his tail. "I feel I have taken up too much of your time."

"This is what my time is for." Bakr smiled. "But I won't keep you. Please do call on me if you wish to talk again, and I would very much enjoy seeing you at one of our group meetings. I did send you the times in the e-mail?"

"Yes." Aziz stood. "I don't know if I'm ready for a large group. But thank you for the talk. I have…much to think about."

Outside, he looked up at the clouds moving across the sky and breathed in the warm air. The day felt more open to him now. The past and present are contained in the future, he thought as he walked down the street. He'd never quite looked at the world that way, and he found it hopeful, if not liberating. The idea that he could maybe one day talk to his son, let alone that his faith could be broad enough to allow for homosexuality beneath its aegis, seemed still as remote as the clouds themselves. But gradually, perhaps, he could change his course.

He stopped on a cool, shady street with an antique store and a vintage clothing shop next to each other. Beside them was an empty storefront, small, with a real estate agent's number on it.

Aziz stared at it. His recent days had been full of signs and portents. Was this another? He took out his phone and noted down the number and then walked on, through Cottage Hill and back to Upper Devos and his own soon-to-be-empty store.

Chapter Fourteen: Separation

"Whoo!" Doug sauntered into the pawnshop and bent his head to the straw in the drink he carried, the plastic cup dripping with condensation. "It's a scorcher today."

Aziz looked up from his computer and smiled. "Summer's in full swing. You closed the store today?"

"All shuttered and the last box off to Tenpenny. I'll go over there next week in case they need help unpacking, but I'm no longer a business owner." The squirrel took in the half-empty pawnshop. "How much longer do you have here?"

"They gave me until the end of July. It's not like I have a place in Coronado to move into by the first."

"Yeah, sorry." Doug leaned against an empty shelf and smiled. "It's been so humid the last few days, I can't wait another week to get out there, much less a month and a half. I can manage the money as well from there as from here."

The payments from Vorvarts were going through banks and lawyers and escrows, and would be parceled out over the next year. There were—necessarily, Aziz and Halifa's lawyer had assured them—plenty of safeguards in place for both parties should something go wrong with the plans. But Vorvarts had put up the money and as of yesterday the first payment had been released from their escrow account, so that was a positive sign.

"Yes." Aziz smiled. "It will be better for me to be here this summer. But I'll come visit you in the fall."

"I still don't know why you'd want to stay here instead of coming out to Coronado. You're used to managing remotely anyway. Just Skype or e-mail. You can work from anywhere."

"I'm changing enough about my life." Aziz looked down at the mail he'd received that day. "The divorce is almost finalized."

Doug sipped from his drink again. "Are you happy?"

"Stop asking me that. Yes, I'm fine."

The squirrel shook his head. "Not the same thing. You're splitting but you're not coming out with me. Losing someone you care about...no matter how you feel now, that's hard."

"We are both moving toward the life we want, and while it is hard to let go, we understand that those lives do not include each other." He flattened his ears. "We will be performing the ceremony at the mosque tonight."

"A ceremony? Is that usual?" Doug waved a paw around. "In front of all those people? You guys take marriage seriously."

"It is very much not usual." Aziz coughed. "Most divorces we know are performed very quietly. But because there is the community here, and..." He looked out the window to the blue glass reflections. "We wanted people to understand, to know, and to not be sad for us. It was Halifa's idea, but I think it is a good one. After all, our faith tells us to think of our fellows above all. Why not allow them to witness this?"

"I guess." Doug took another drink. "Are you going to do another ceremony for your non-Muslim friends?"

Aziz shook his head slowly. "That's why I didn't tell you before."

"Oh well." The squirrel flashed a bucktoothed smile. "You're coming to my going-away party, though, right?"

"Of course."

Doug flipped idly through the last twelve DVDs in the bin without looking at them. Fingers still on the cases, he raised his eyes, his expression more serious. "So tell me something. She's going to do her charities, right? What about you? You keep saying you're going to 'figure it out.' But you're no closer to telling me what you're doing than you were a month ago."

"I haven't figured it out yet." He smiled. "But I feel certain Allah will provide."

Doug chuckled. "Well, I can't argue. You seem happier lately, like the store was a weight lifted off your back."

"Something like that perhaps." Aziz looked past Doug, out the window past the sign that said "SALES ONLY — NOTHING BOUGHT" to the bright storefronts across the street. "I've been feeling more sorry for the people losing their place here, but there's nothing more I can do at this point."

"You're doing all you can." Doug walked up to the counter, looking over it for Aziz's trash bin. The cheetah held it up and Doug dropped his drink into it. "That's another reason I'm leaving. I don't want to see it die. I'll have my family out in Coronado and that'll have to be enough."

"It will be."

The squirrel remained by the counter, searching Aziz's eyes. "You still haven't called him?"

The cheetah shook his head. "I don't know what I'd say."

"You know how to start. Don't worry about the rest."

"I know." He placed his paws on the glass below which was displayed only one tarnished silver necklace. "But it's so difficult."

Doug reached over to pat him on the shoulder. "Trust yourself. Let go of the past."

"Easy for you to say. You sold your past so you could run away from it."

"I'm not running away so fast you couldn't catch me if you wanted to." The squirrel grinned.

"I'll come out often, if I can afford it. My money will be tied up for the first year or two."

"I'll buy you a ticket, then."

"Deal." Aziz stuck out a paw. "See you Thursday night."

"You bet." Doug grasped and squeezed the offered paw. "All right. Hey, it's about your tea time, isn't it?"

"Is it?" Aziz turned to the space where the grandfather clock had been and then looked down at his phone. "So it is."

"I'm going to get on home and start packing. Good luck tonight, huh?"

"Thank you." Aziz raised a paw and watched his friend's bushy tail flick back and forth as he stepped out into the glow of the afternoon and disappeared past the window. Then he took out his samovar and sat at the end of his nearly-empty counter.

الْوَقْتِ الَّذِيْ يُرِيْدُ

A few of the males and females gathered together after their prayer in the community room on the second floor of the mosque. Aziz and Halifa stood at the center, holding each other's paws. She wore her green and yellow scarf over her head and ears, and Aziz wore the shirt he'd brought from Madiyah, the one Halifa had mended several times and later taken to be repaired several more. As he felt the warmth of her paws in his and studied her golden eyes, Aziz felt moved to speak. "I've cherished the years of our marriage and the friendship we've grown between us," he said. "This is not an expression of regret for the past, but of understanding of the future."

"We'll remain friends," Halifa said. Her paws squeezed his lightly. "You have been an excellent husband and partner, and I look forward to our separate futures."

He smiled and opened his mouth. The words stuck, difficult to say even though he could hear them in his head. He saw before him their marriage ceremony in the courtyard of his father's house, the bright sun over their heads, the greenery and flowers all around against the yellow sandstone of the house, all the guests cheering as he and Halifa joined their lives together. He saw them in the cool strangeness of the airplane with only one suitcase each, stepping off a bus into a loud, smelly morass of people in Upper Devos. Sanding and painting the shop, working with the numbers in paper books and later on computers, traveling to the beach with their son, going to see him play tennis, all the pieces of their lives together to that point. The future, he reminded himself, contains the past. And also the present.

"I divorce you. I divorce you. I divorce you," he said, and released her paws.

She bowed her head. "I divorce you," she repeated three times, even though the wife was not required to say the words.

Then she bowed, for physical contact between them was no longer proper, and the small crowd around them murmured their blessings. When they broke apart, the females came forward to take Halifa to them, and the males came forward for Aziz.

Marris came up to him first. "Salaam," he said, and Aziz returned the greeting. "I'm hopeful this new life you're beginning will be good for you."

"Thank you. And thank you for coming to witness."

"I haven't seen a divorce celebrated before."

"And?"

Marris tilted his head, thinking. "I believe I like it. You're letting us know it's desired by both parties." He smiled. "We're all of us servants of Allah, no?"

"Yes." Aziz swept his ears back. "I heard about your apartment building today. I'm sorry. Do you have another place?"

The red fox nodded. "Out in Sun Terrace. It will be a longer ride to work, but at least it's a home. I can still come here most days in the evening before going home."

"I'm glad to hear it."

Marris bowed his head, his ears settling back. "I did not take any of your generous gift to the mosque. I can afford to move. There are others not so lucky."

"Don't hesitate to ask Ashtari if you run into extra expenses. That happens a lot when you move. I promise, there's enough to go around."

From him, Aziz moved on to talk with the others. None of them blamed him to his face for the development, but below the pleasant conversation he sensed a distance still there, and there were some who'd chosen not to come to the ceremony at all. He had chosen to give up his home and business and been paid well for it, so whether they held him accountable or not, he wasn't facing the same problems they were. Some of them saw the money he and Halifa had contributed—a tenth of what they'd received from Vorvarts—as an attempt to expiate their guilt rather than Islamic charity.

"Look at it like a natural disaster," Halifa said when he brought this up in the car. Technically speaking, he should not be in the company of an unrelated, unaccompanied female, but when he'd suggested he could take a cab to his apartment, Halifa had told him to get in the car, that she would drive him, and none of the bystanders had even looked bothered. "A tornado ravages the community, leaving behind soulless conglomerations of identical housing and corporate shops. You hope it's not your community, but if it is, you make the best of it."

"That absolves the people behind the decisions. Nobody tells the tornado where to land, but they choose where to send the bulldozers."

"Yes," she said, "but we're not talking about them. We're talking about us. We can no more affect what buildings they set their sights on than we can tell the sandstorm to turn back. Or the thunderstorm, if you like."

"But we could have fought. We could have made it harder for them."

"And gained what, in the end? They have money and power. Better to put our energies toward rebuilding our communities where we can. You and I, we've been through enough change to know that change isn't only an ending. It's a beginning."

Of course it was, he thought as he fitted the unfamiliar key into the door of his apartment. And yet, he would miss his house, the old wood railings on the staircase, the creaky step he'd learned to avoid. He would miss the smells that had accumulated over time and the particularly crooked way the door hung in his doorway—not enough to keep it from closing, but enough to let light in near the top. He would miss Halifa, of course, but they would remain close; dissolving their marriage and their business partnership wouldn't end their friendship.

The future might be unknown, unknowable, but by choosing the parts of his past that he chose to bring forward into it, he could at least control some of its shape. He might not know where he would live, but he would have Doug and Halifa and Gerald as friends. He would have his possessions: the tea service, the rugs, the clothing he loved. He would have his tail and his ears and the ache in his back.

Perhaps it was all the things that were leaving his life that made him think of one that had already left. Or maybe it was the words of Gerald and Bakr and most of all Halifa that had allowed him to open the door he'd thought closed forever. He had not forgotten, would never forget, the words his son had spoken. But he could choose to leave those in the past and bring the parts of his son that he loved with him into the future.

He sat on the bed in his new room beside the suitcase he hadn't yet unpacked and took out his phone. The name "Marquize" glowed up at him over ten digits and the picture of an old phone receiver, like the kind they'd had when they'd first moved to the States.

He said a short *du'a* to ask for favorable outcomes—to ask for the patience and love he should have had years ago. Then he touched the phone icon and brought the phone to his ear.

Epilogue

The chill of winter still lingered in the air outside, but the flowers blooming in the window planters outside the pastry shop assured Aziz that spring was not far away. Beyond them, he recognized Halifa's figure crossing the street, checking her phone, and then looking up and spotting the shop. He smiled and took a sip of his tea, listening to the busy murmur of all the people sitting at tables, talking, checking their laptops. His own phone was open to the text messages with Gerald; the cougar said he had a friend Aziz might like and Aziz was trying to figure out how to reply. The whole conversation had rekindled his apprehension about how today would go. Would he have enough strength and inner peace? He hoped so; he had prayed for those qualities every day for the past three weeks.

A few moments later, the bell on the door tinkled and Halifa entered. Aziz rose to his feet. "I'm so glad you made it."

"Oh, I wouldn't have missed it." She adjusted her scarf. "It's very busy. You've done a good job promoting it. I saw several people talking about it."

"I hired a young fellow from the mosque. He's much more adept with social media than I am. Has a Twitter…is that right? And Insta…"

"Instagram," Halifa supplied, still smiling. She stepped up to the counter. "Hello, Tanska. The new shop is lovely."

"Hmph." The tiger glanced at Aziz. "It's smaller."

"It's actually fifty square feet larger," Aziz told Halifa.

"This counter is larger. Too big." Halifa swept her paws across it. "And I don't need all this space behind it."

"When it's two people back there, you will." Aziz brushed the gleaming amber surface. "This is polished marble from Siberia."

"It's lovely," Halifa said.

"It's heavy." Tanska grunted. "I strained my back lifting it."

"I told you to let the workers do it." Aziz turned to Halifa. "She's very particular when it comes to her store."

"I know how I like things done." The tiger made another "hmph" noise. "This one thinks he knows best. Pawnshops aren't pastry shops."

"He knows a lot," Halifa said. "You two work very well together. Now…" She examined the case. "Oh, it must be the rosewater and pistachio crescents, no?"

Aziz stood a little straighter, his chest puffed out. "Yes."

"They are palatable," Tanska admitted grudgingly. "He is not bad with dough."

"I looked up a recipe online and Tanska helped me work it with her ingredients." Aziz smiled. "Sort of a present reimagining of the past."

"I like that. One, please, and a mint tea."

Tanska plated the pastry and poured the tea, but when she placed them on the counter, she refused Halifa's money. "Aziz always said you talked him into staying in this area, so I owe you at least one meal."

Halifa turned, her smile getting wider. "I didn't talk him into anything. He chose to educate himself and to discover what he valued and wanted to preserve from his life."

"Don't be modest," Aziz said. "Take the free pastry."

"Thank you," Halifa said, putting her wallet away. "And thank you, Tanska. Congratulations again on the new shop."

"It only has two years of funding," the tiger said. "Most likely we'll go out of business."

"Then we'll figure something else out." Aziz gestured back toward his table. "Let's sit down before Tanska starts crying over her new store."

"We're farther from the subway," she called after them before attending to the next customer.

"Was she like that the whole last year?" Halifa asked as they sat.

"More or less." Aziz smiled. "In private, with beer, she loosens up somewhat. And when we were focused on the work of getting this done, she was all business."

"It's a good shop. It'll succeed."

"I think so. The real estate agent picked this location because the frontage is very good. That's what she said. It faces an open intersection so you can see it from there, there, there." He pointed out the window down all three nearby streets. "And it's got a little upstairs space that we're going to turn into an area for local clubs or groups to use. Still working on that."

Halifa bit the end off the crescent pastry. "It's so nice to see you this excited."

"It has been a lot of fun. Work, too, but…" Aziz nodded, his eyes on the pastry. "How do you like it?"

"Lovely. I didn't know you could bake. I wish you'd baked more while we were married."

"I never knew I could either, until I tried." Aziz settled his elbows on the table.

She looked toward the register and the pastry case. "Will you be helping Tanska behind the counter here as well?"

"I did this morning." He put a paw to his back, still sore from all the standing, but it was a soreness he took pride in. "We hired a ferret to work but he quit right before we opened. We just hired a wolf, Marta, she's going to college nearby, but she's out of town today and couldn't get back. Mostly I want to sit here and watch the flowers and the people, and help Tanska run the business."

"Well, thank you for inviting me to see it. I would've come anyway, but it was nice to be thought of." She finished the pastry and licked her fingers clean.

Aziz had spotted another familiar figure coming down the street. "There's actually another reason I invited you today," he said.

"Oh?" She turned to follow him with her eyes as he stood and made his way to the door.

A skunk came in, and then a short Prevost's squirrel with a soft beach shirt draped over his chest. "Zeez!"

"Doug!" They embraced, and Aziz gestured toward Halifa. "Halifa's here too."

"Ah, it's good to see you again." Doug hurried over to where Halifa was standing, and embraced her as well.

"Coronado looks good on you," Aziz said, remaining by the door.

Doug patted his stomach. "I've brought ten pounds of it back with me. When you lie around on the beach all day, well… Anyway, Kev's gotten me started walking for a couple hours a day. You two look as good as ever."

"It's so lovely to see you." Halifa's eyes met Aziz's, and he knew the question she was asking. Doug had been much more Aziz's friend than hers; was this the reason? He looked outside, but the sidewalk was clear.

And then a tall cheetah in a Rage Against t-shirt and threadbare jeans scuffed his way past the front windows and hesitated at the door. Behind him, a short bobcat pushing a stroller leaned forward to say something to him. The cheetah turned and replied, then caught sight of Aziz waiting and took a step back.

Halifa caught sight of him. "Aziz, is that…?" She hurried out the door to grasp her son by the paw.

"He almost didn't get on the plane," Doug said under his breath to Aziz. "Colin," he nodded to the bobcat, "and I had to drag him on. For a minute I was worried they'd think we were kidnapping him."

Mother and son embraced out on the sidewalk and then came back to the doorway, followed by the bobcat and the stroller. Again, Marquize hesitated, looking in at his father.

And Aziz felt all the shards of their broken past coming together neatly in the present, bound by Allah's peace and love into a great swell of gratitude for the chance at a new future. Relieved, Aziz basked in the glow and held out his arms to his son. "Please," he said, "come in."

About This Book and Islam

This story came to me in the way many stories do: Aziz is a minor character in my novel series *Love Match*, and the topic of gentrification is a hot one in the Bay Area where I live (as it is in Brooklyn, where Upper Devos is modeled and where I visited earlier this year). I wanted to write about a character going through changes, and specifically about an older character making changes later in life. Aziz suggested himself, with the added complexity that the religion that had caused him to reject his gay son was not Christianity but Islam.

I'm not Muslim, and this story is not intended to be an introduction to or primer in Islam. Aziz's religion serves as the foundation of his life and the context in which he forms many of his attitudes, and Islam is presented so that the reader can gain insight into the main character. That said, I am aware that many readers of this book (predominantly American) may have no experience with Muslims or Islam apart from what they see on TV, and so I have tried to be descriptive and at the same time respectful of Islam and Muslims. A Muslim friend was kind enough to read the manuscript and correct many small details of Aziz's life; any mistakes that remain are my oversight and I apologize for them. If you are interested in learning more about Islam, my friend suggests that you start at the site *http://www.whyislam.org/*. And of course, there are as many variations on Islamic culture around the world as there are variations on Christian culture. The specific one represented in this book is only one small (fictional) one (two, counting Aziz's home country).

Another reason to write this book is the plight of gay Muslims, who face the dual problems of homophobia and Islamophobia. There are communities online where queer Muslims gather, and there are ongoing attempts to reconcile queer Muslims with their faith, including the work of Dr. Scott Siraj al-Haqq Kugle (from which I drew much of Bakr's reasoning). If you are queer and Muslim, there are others like you and places you can go.

Acknowledgments

Many thanks are due to Dwale, who provided feedback on the life of Muslims and on Islamic culture both in reviewing the text and in several conversations. I'm indebted to him for opening up about his life and faith to me.

Thanks of course to my writing group: Ryan Campbell, David Cowan, and Watts Martin. Their continuing friendship and feedback have been invaluable to my books. And thanks to Malcolm Cross, who also reviewed this text and co-founded the Cupcake line with me.

Thanks also to FurPlanet Productions and FuzzWolf in particular for their willingness to take a chance on a non-traditional story and point of view.

And of course, thanks to Jack and Kit for their continuing support in so many ways.

About the Author

Kyell Gold has won twelve Ursa Major awards for his stories and novels, and his acclaimed novel "Out of Position" co-won the Rainbow Award for Best Gay Novel of 2009. His novel "Green Fairy" was nominated for inclusion in the ALA's "Over the Rainbow" list for 2012. He helped create RAWR, the first residential furry writing workshop, and was one of the instructors at its first session in 2016.

He lives in California and loves to travel and dine out with his husband Kit Silver, and can be seen at furry conventions around the world. More information about him and his books is available at *http://www.kyellgold.com.*

About the Artist

Kamui makes his home in the Bay Area, where he enjoys painting fuzzy folk, drawing from life, and taking long walks around town (with lots of stops in eateries along the way). These days, he's joining Aziz in trying to make peace with the changes taking place in his lovely city; the present never sticks around long, but there's new beauty in what tomorrow brings (and new restaurants, too!).

About Cupcakes

Cupcakes are novellas, with more substance than short stories, though not as long as novels. The Cupcakes line was developed for FurPlanet by foozzzball, Kyell Gold, and Rikoshi as a reaction to their desire to tell novella-length stories and the lack of publishing opportunities for novellas.

Previous Cupcakes have been nominated four times for Ursa Major awards, winning twice, and six times for Cóyotl Awards, winning three.

About the Publisher

FurPlanet publishes original works of furry fiction. You can explore their selection at *http://www.furplanet.com* and find their e-books at *http://www.baddogbooks.com*.

Printed in Great Britain
by Amazon

74001595R00071